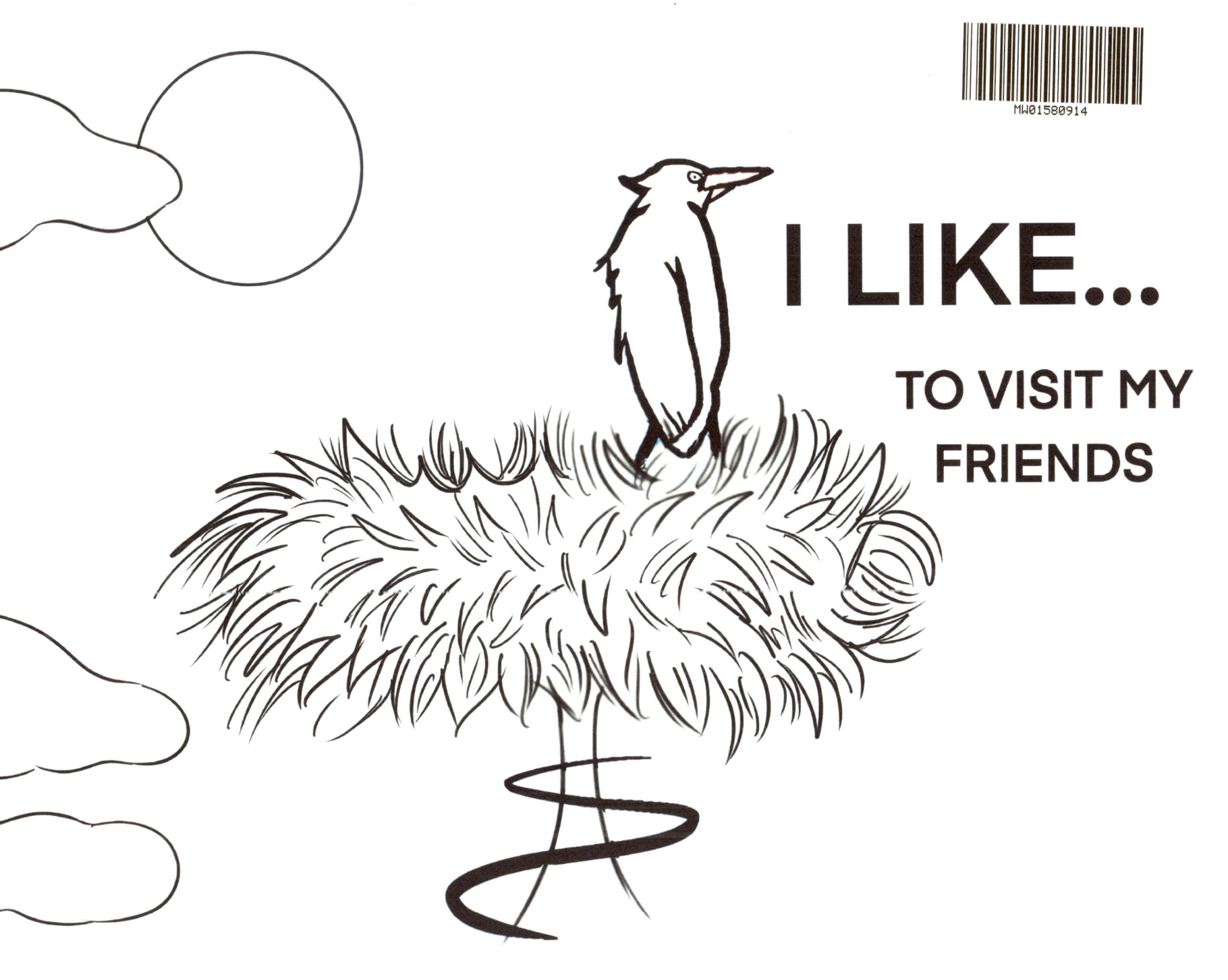

I LIKE...

TO VISIT MY FRIENDS

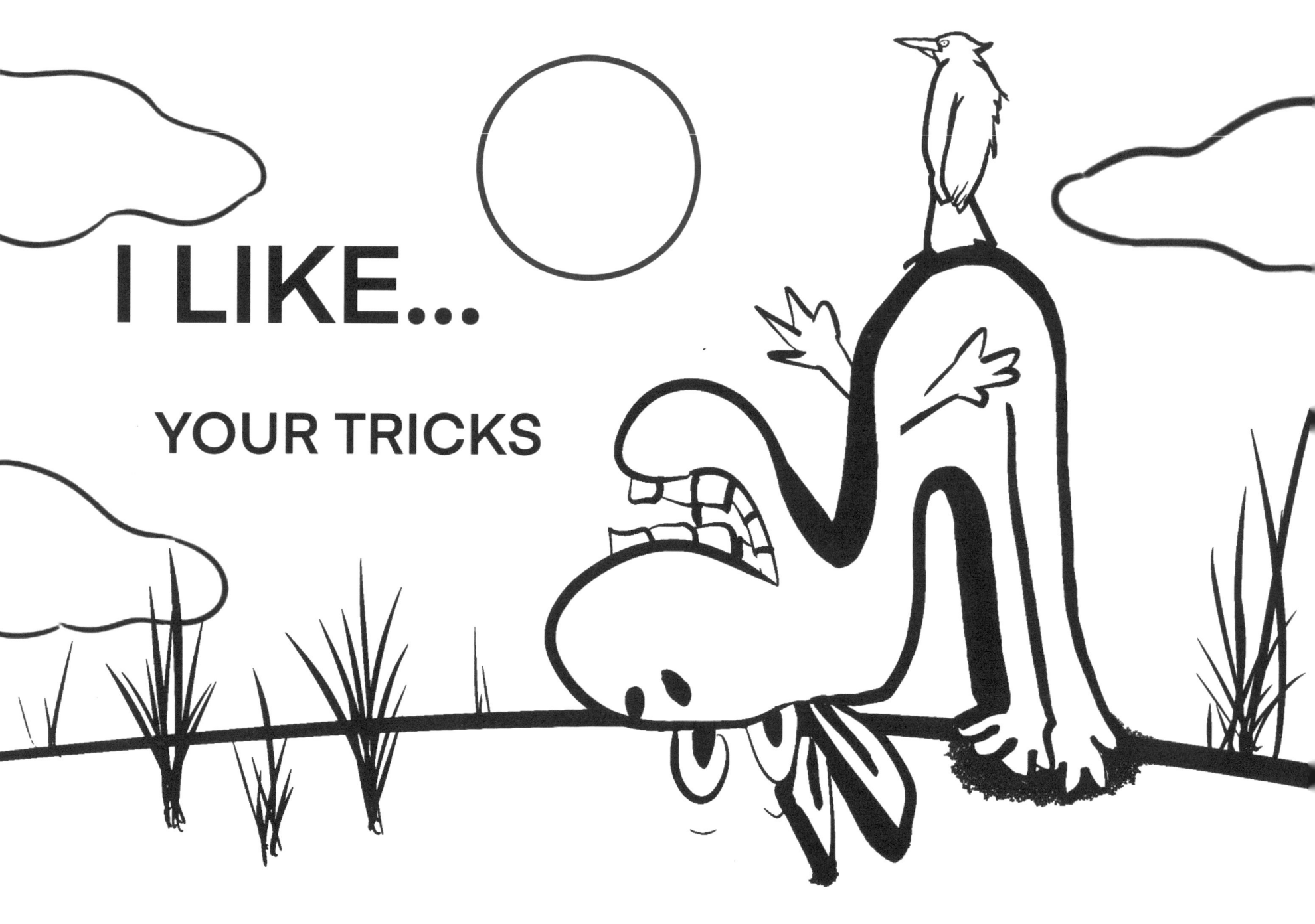

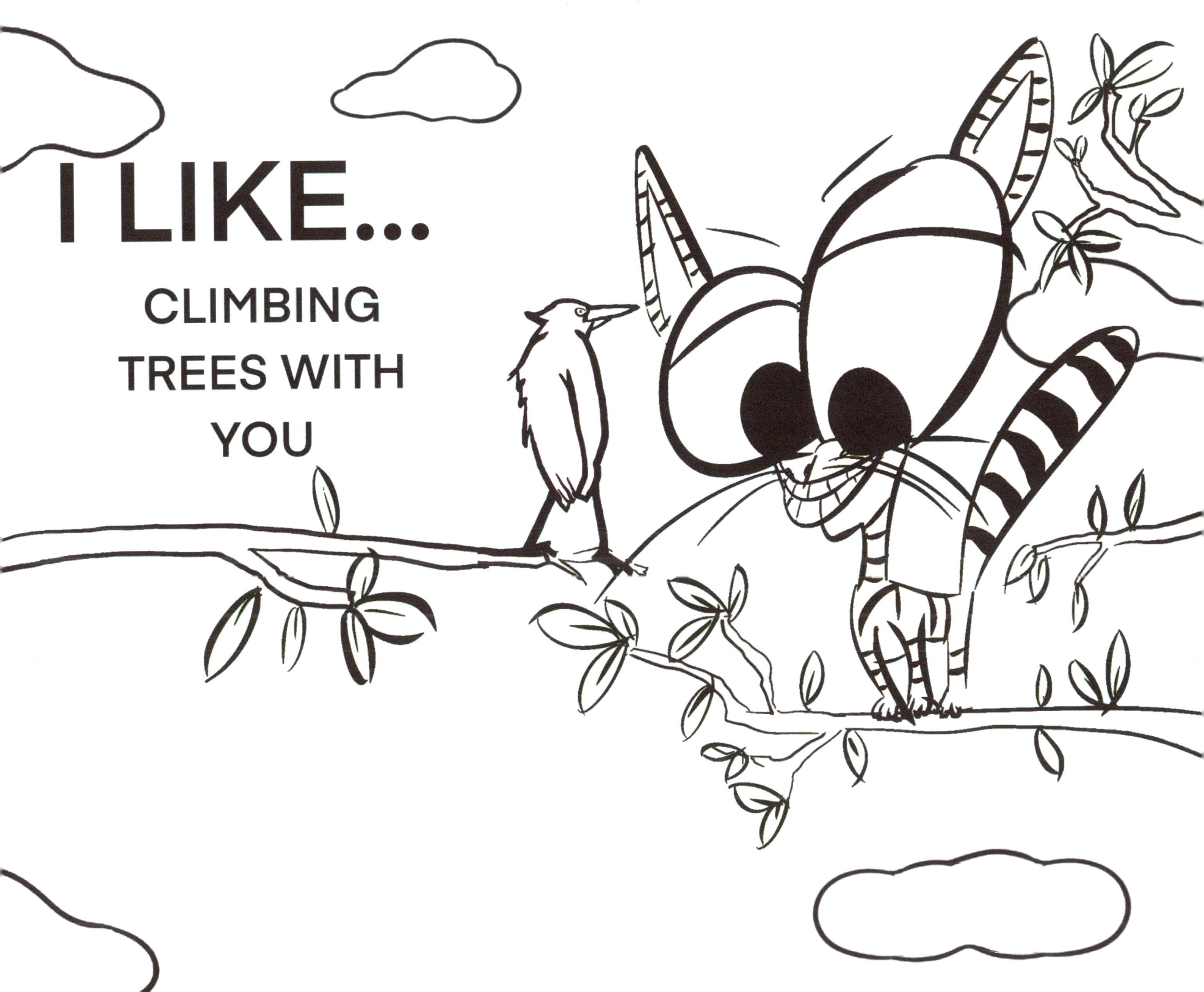

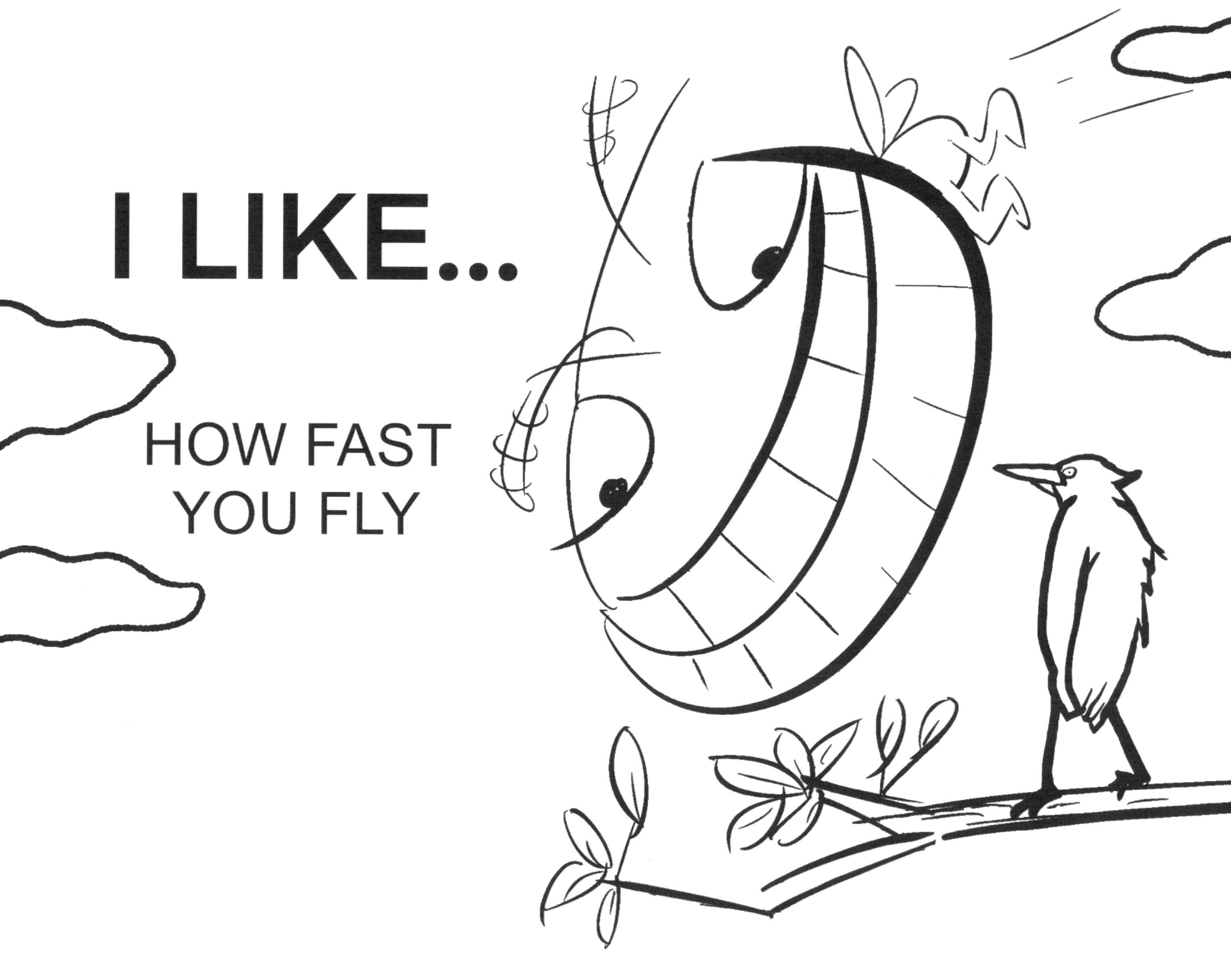

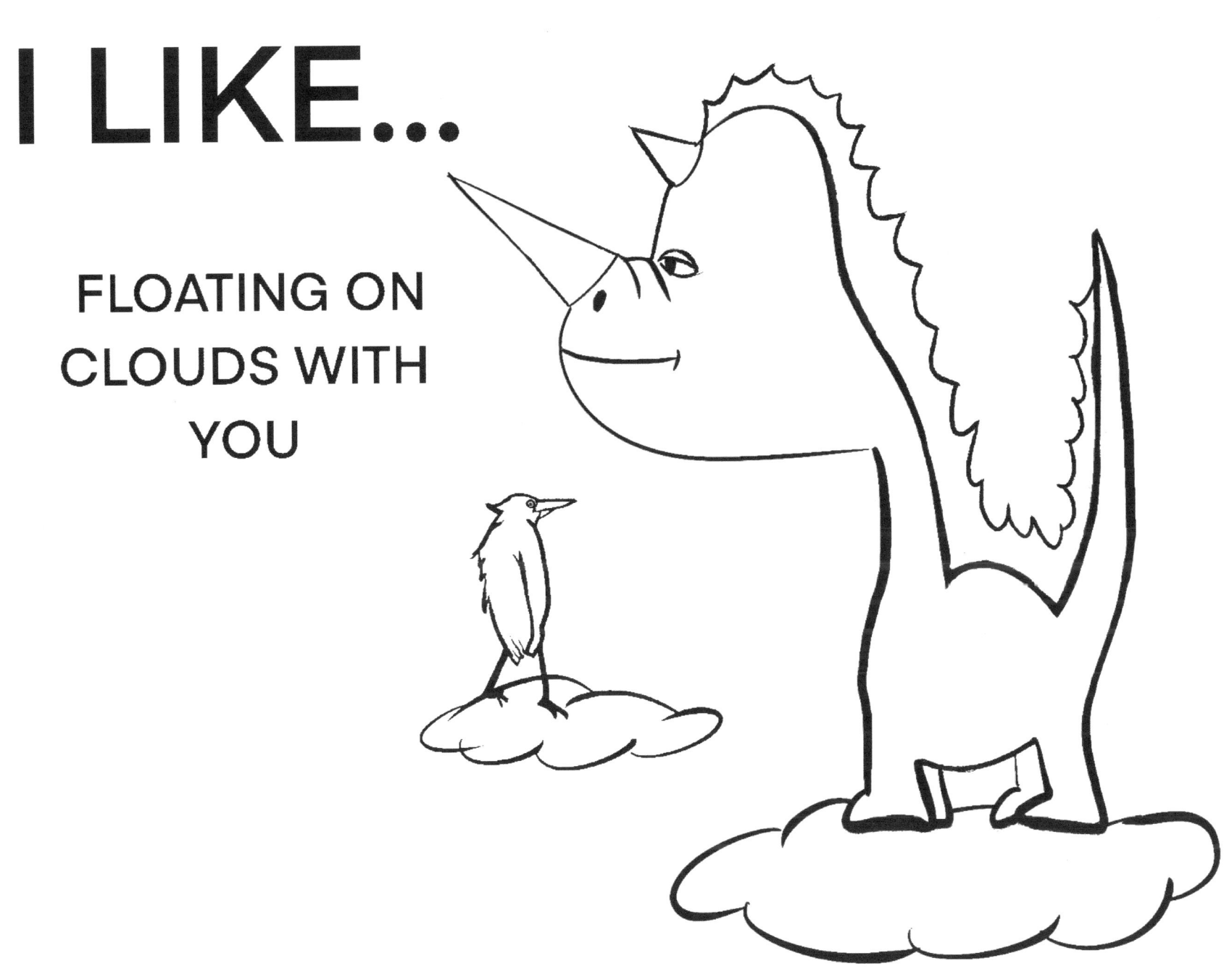

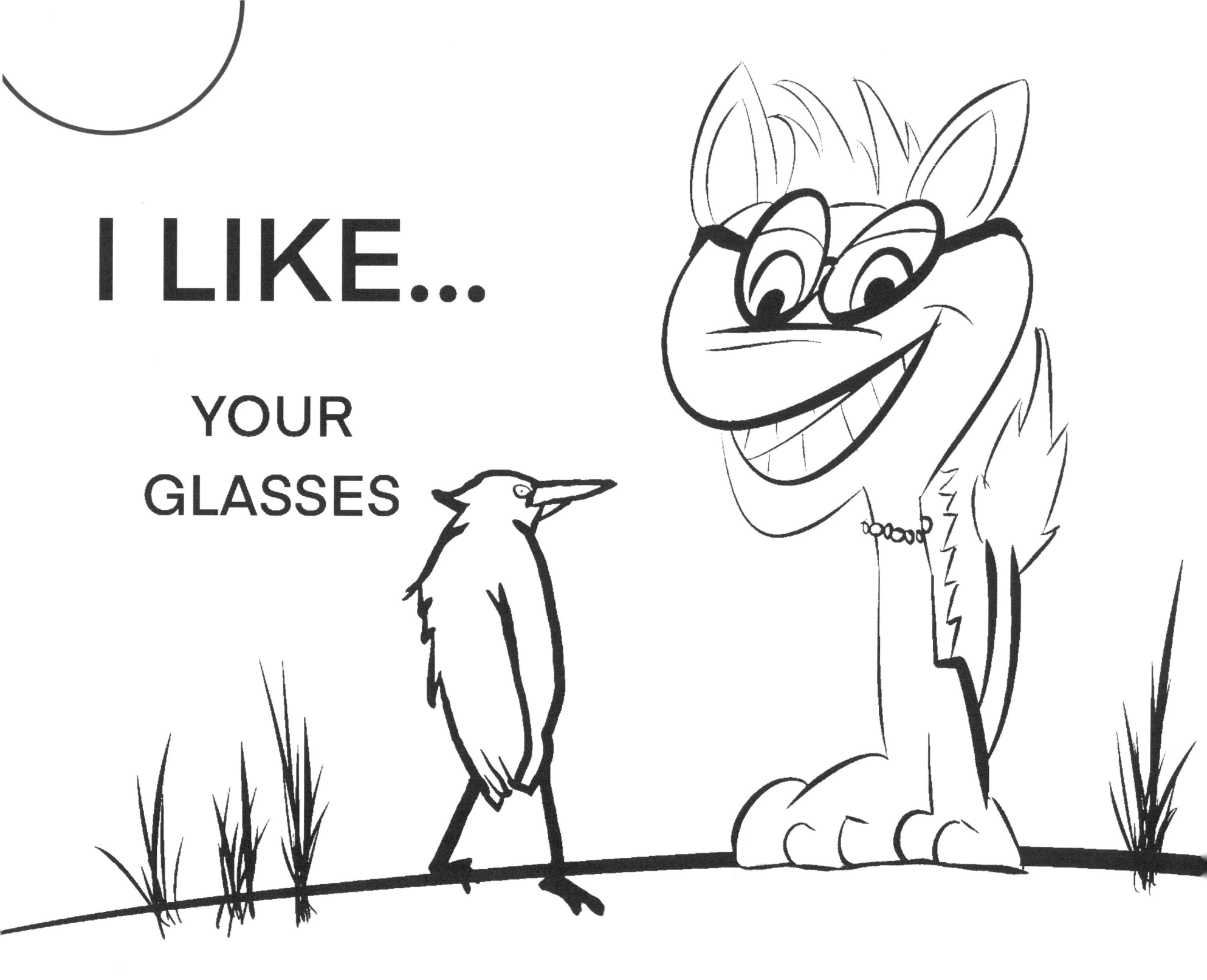

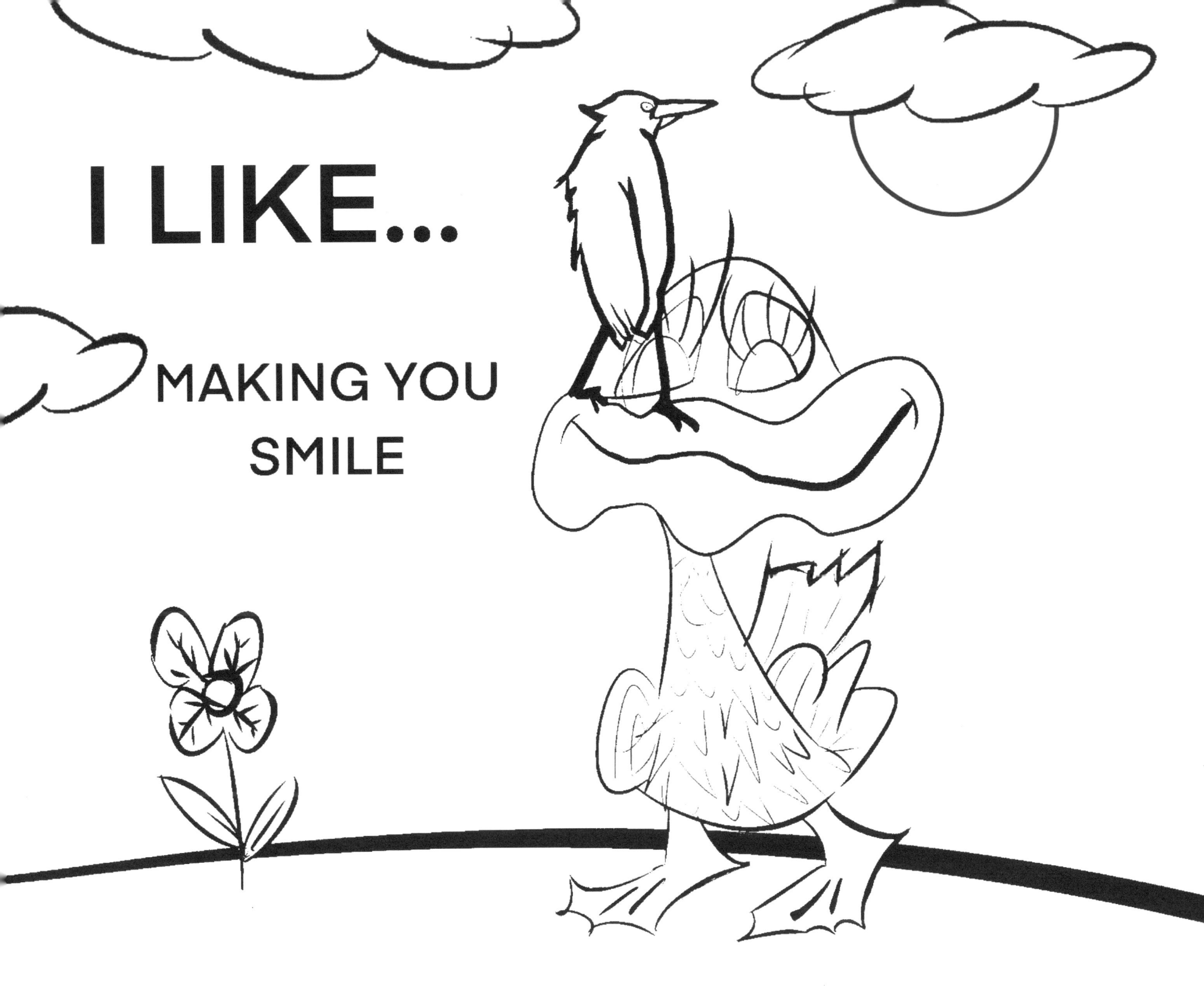

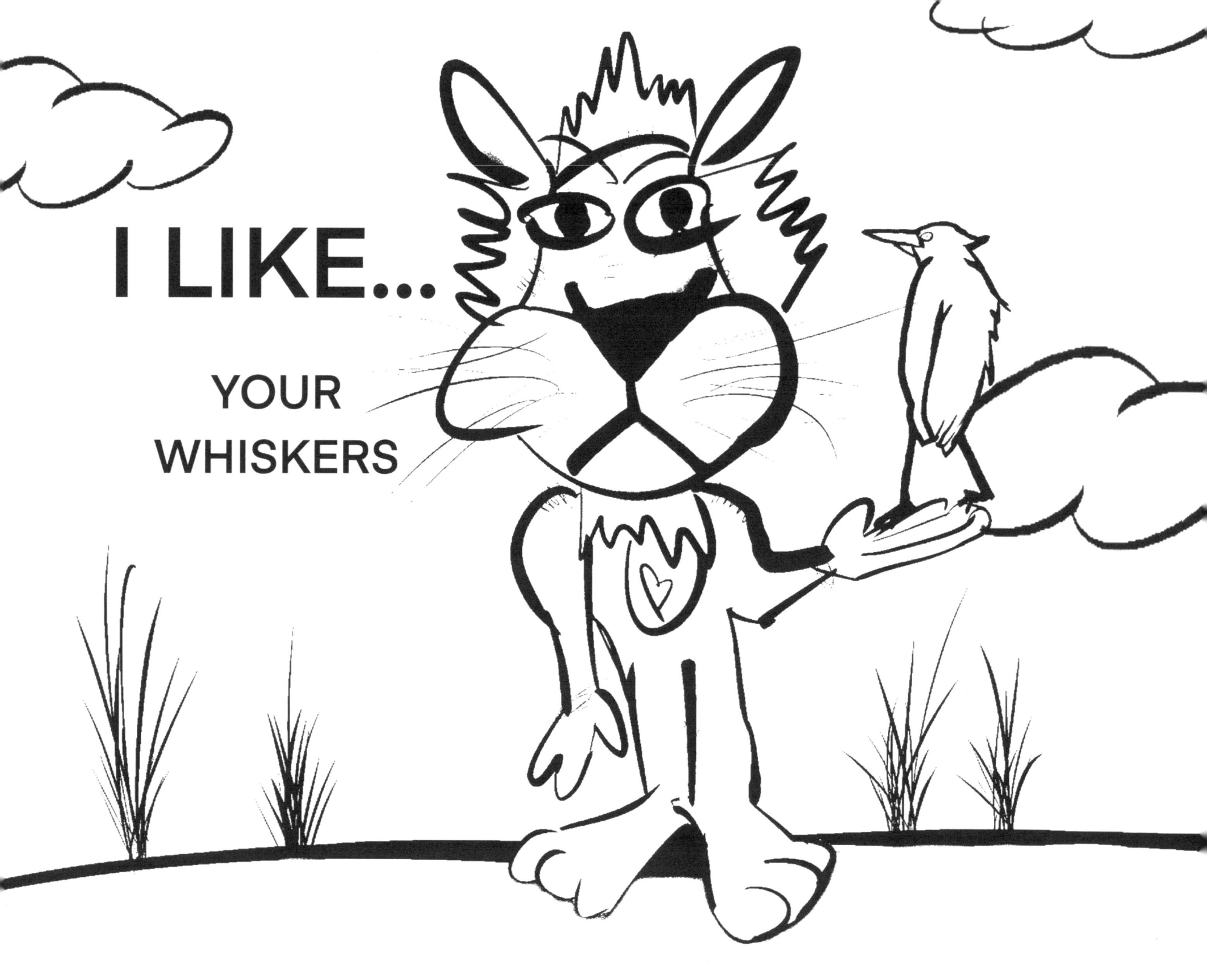

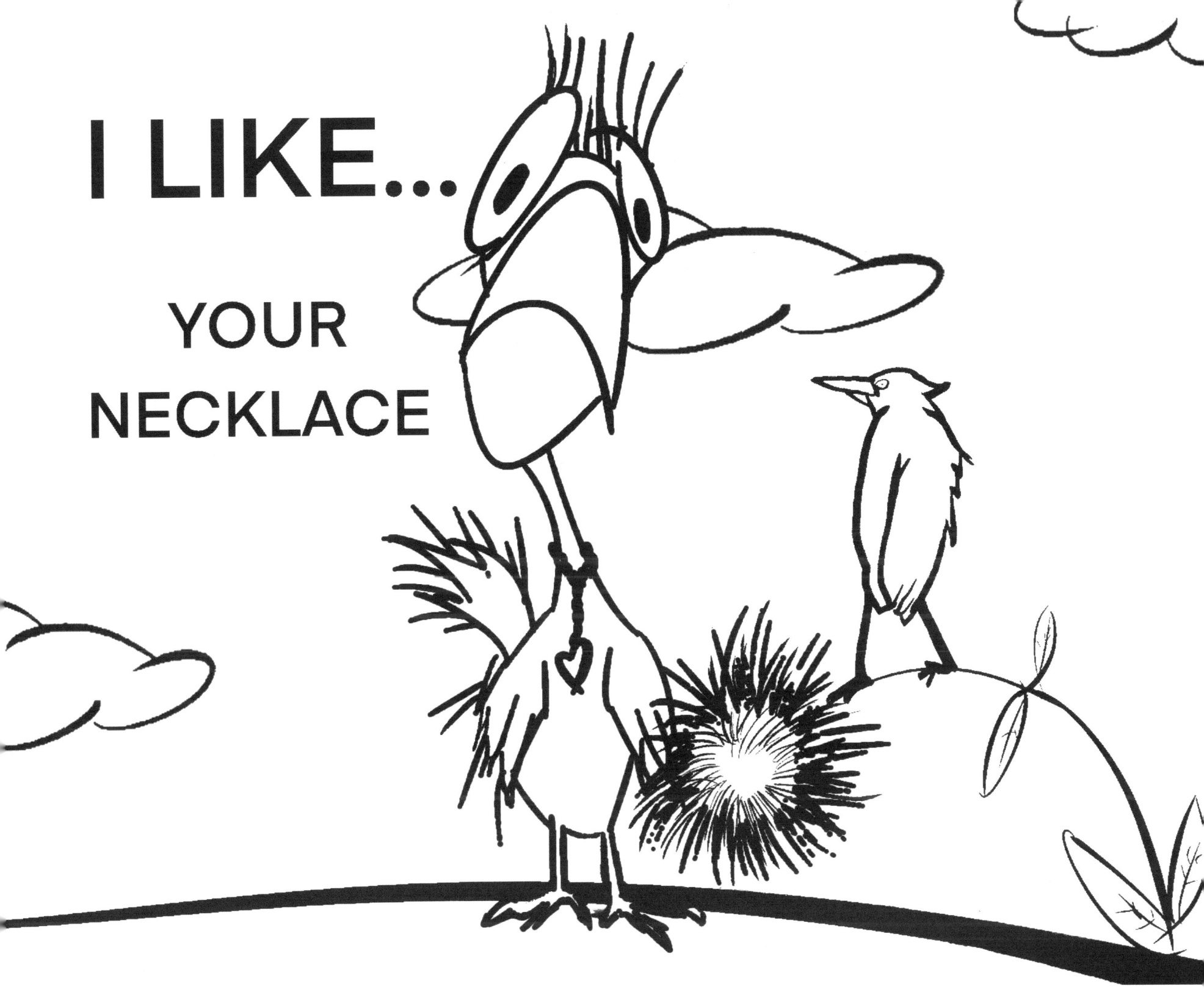

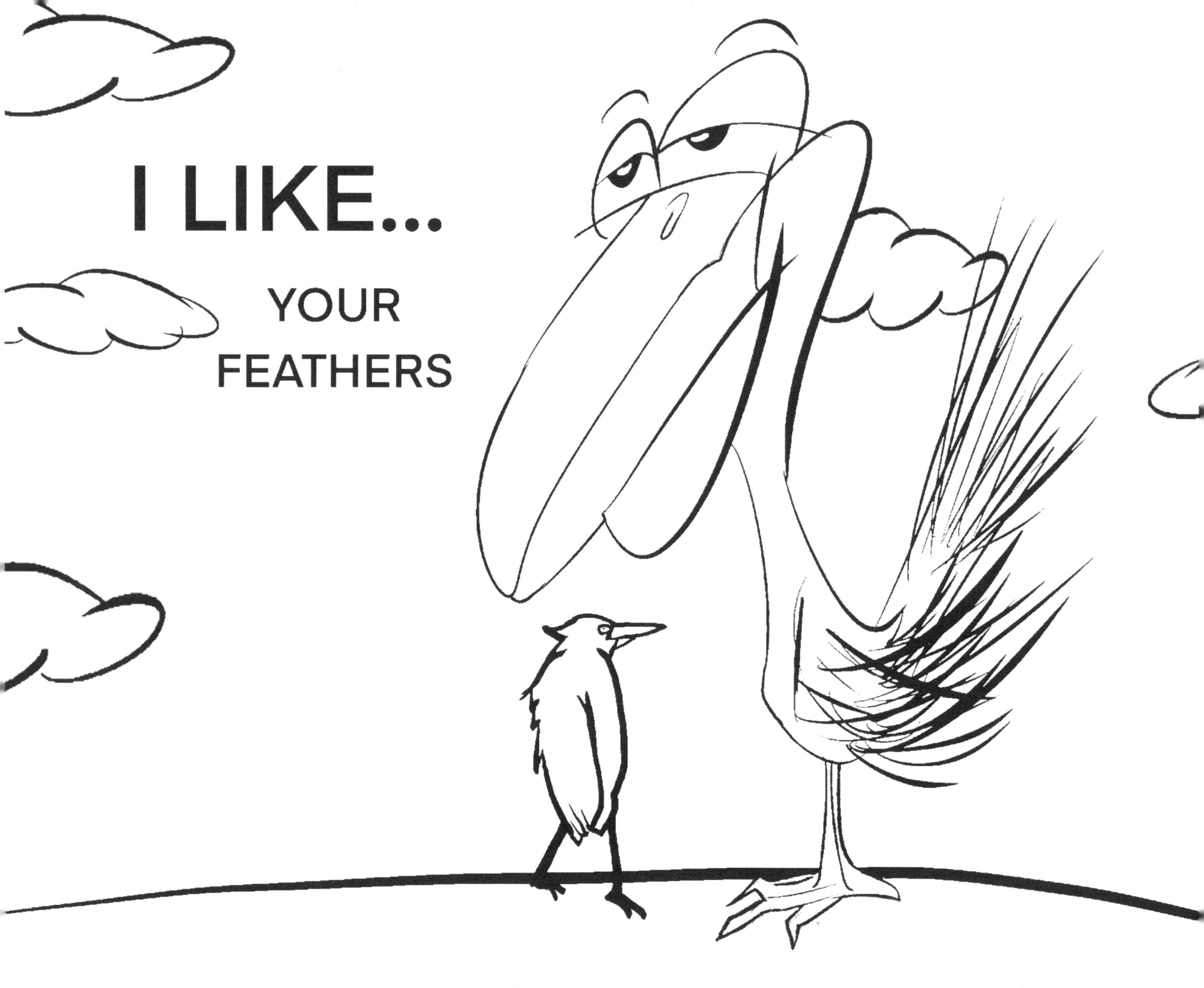

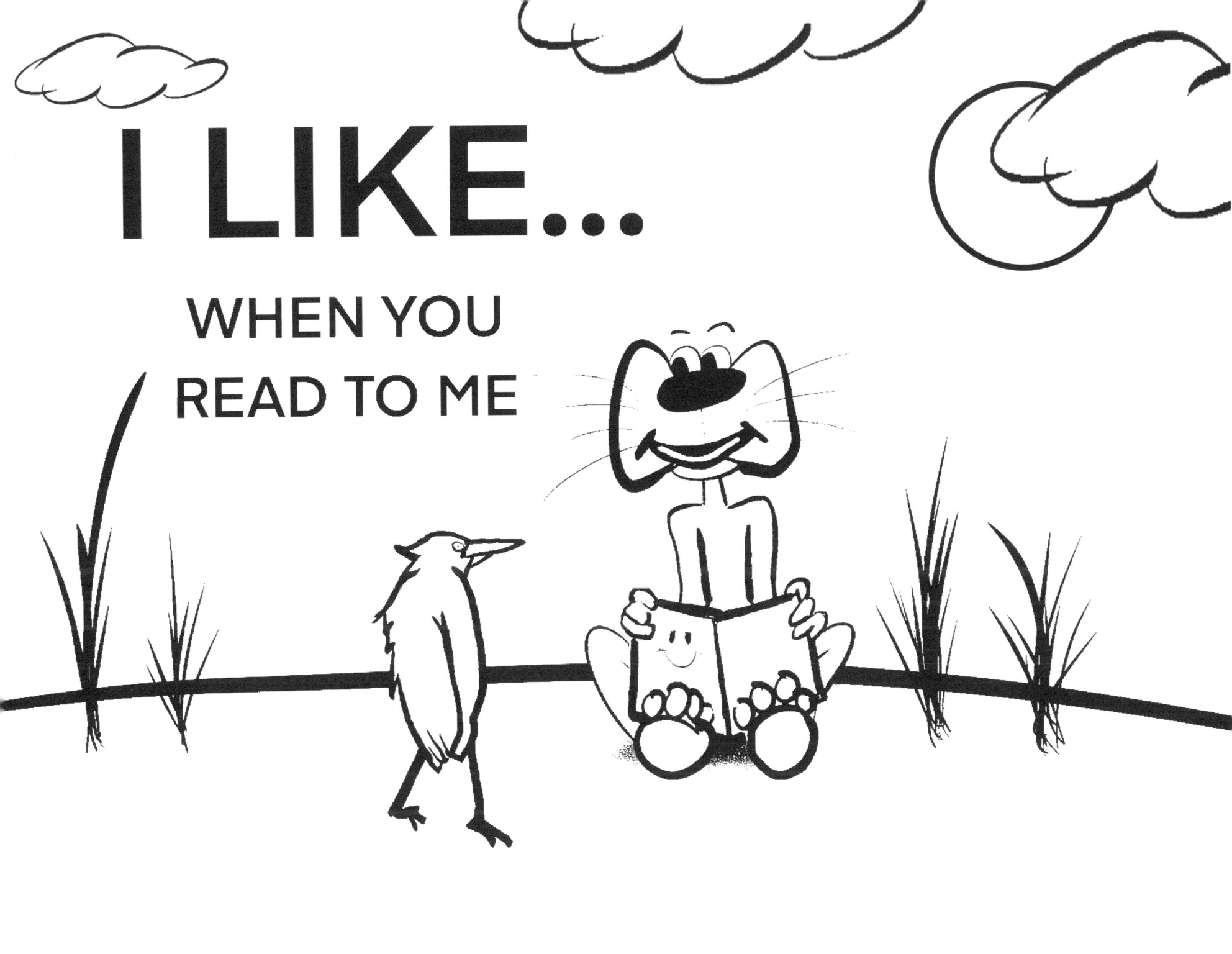

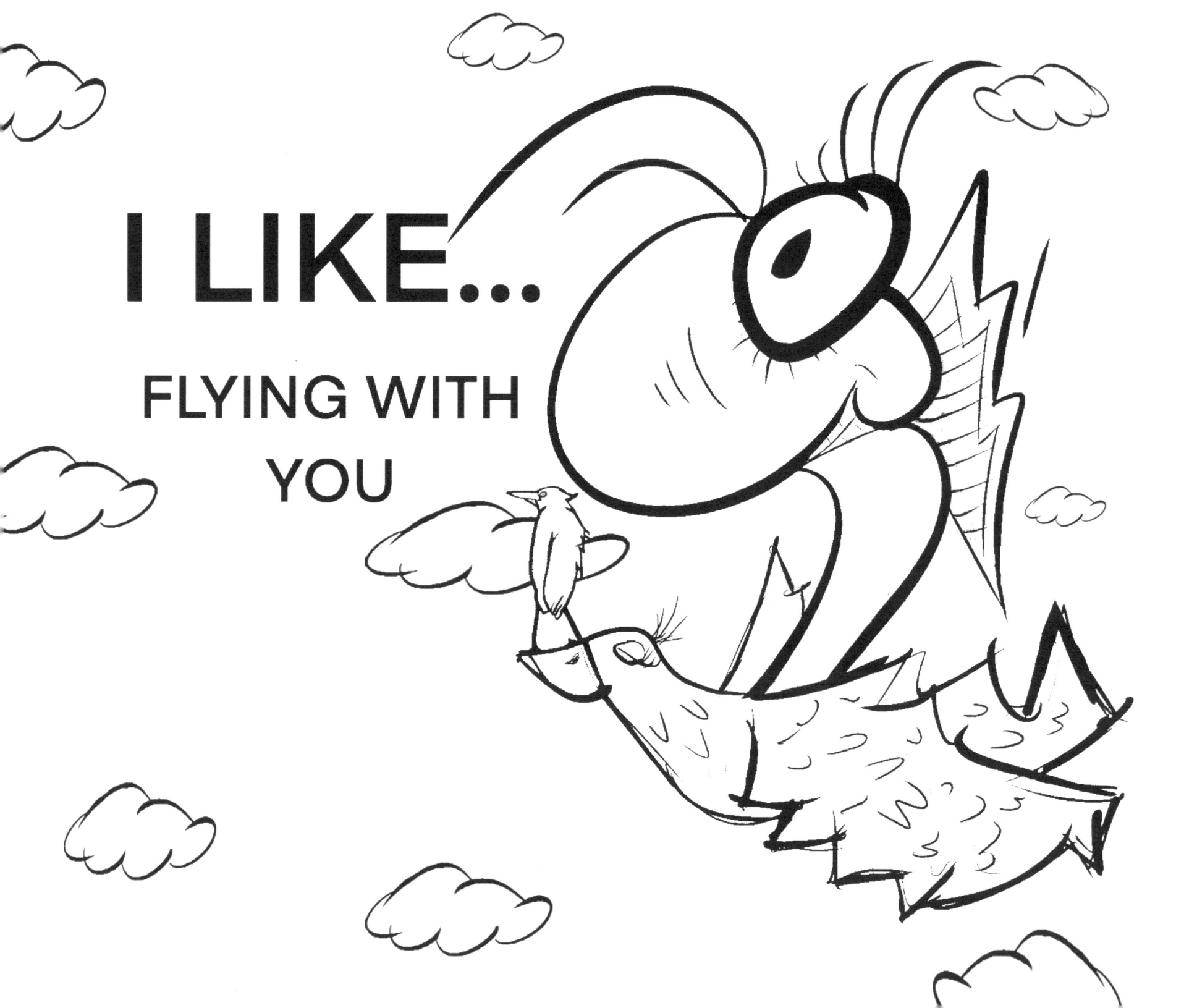

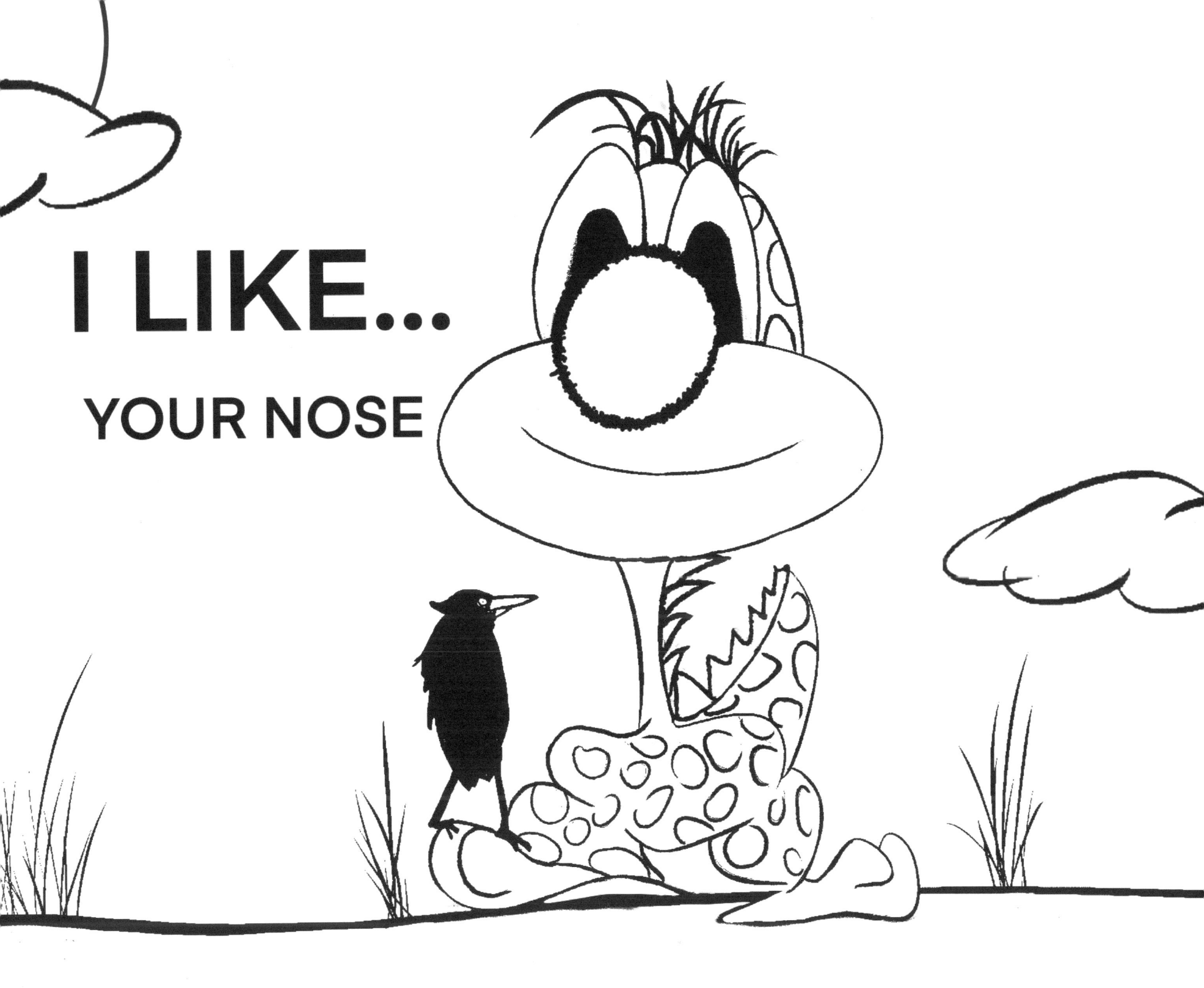

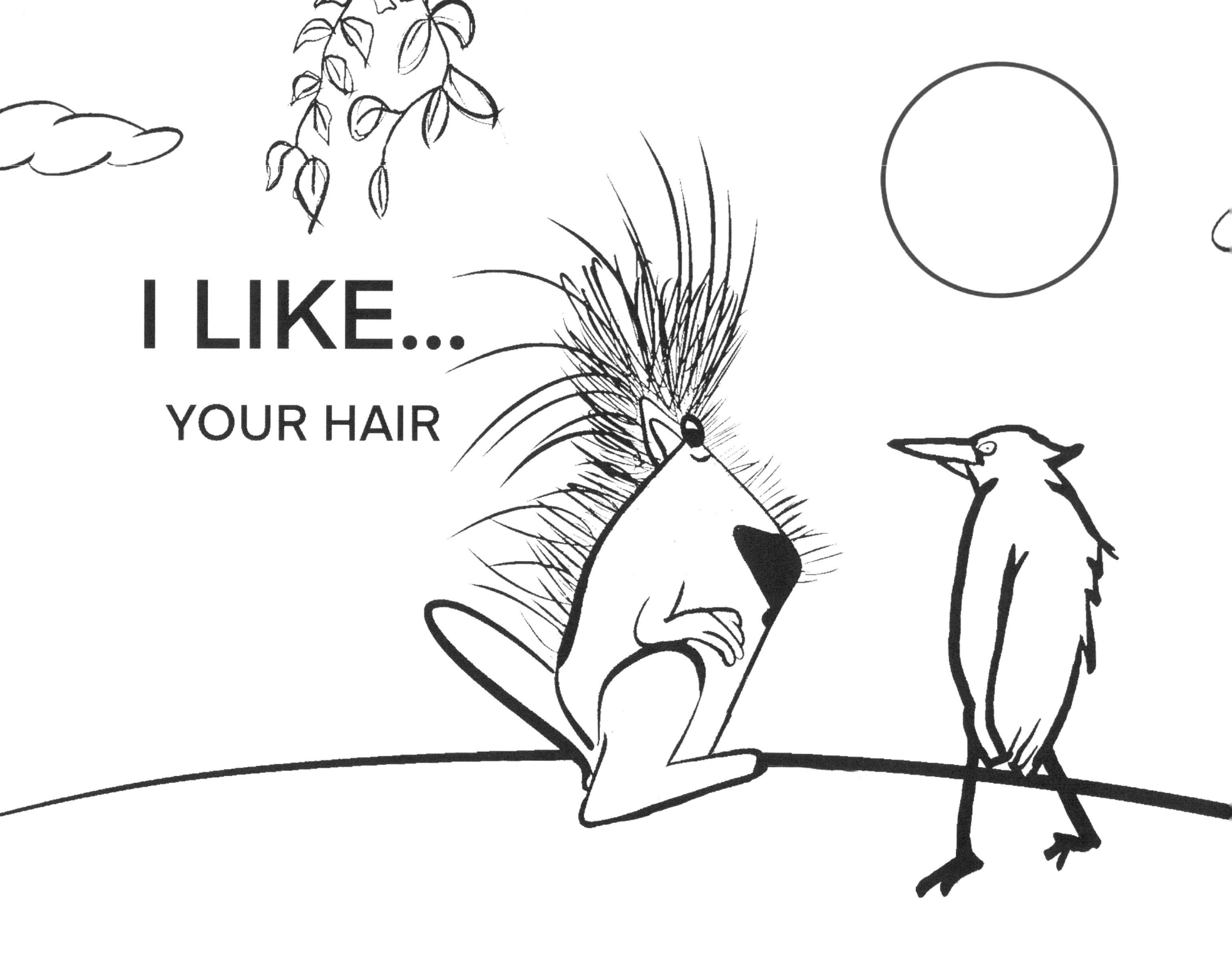

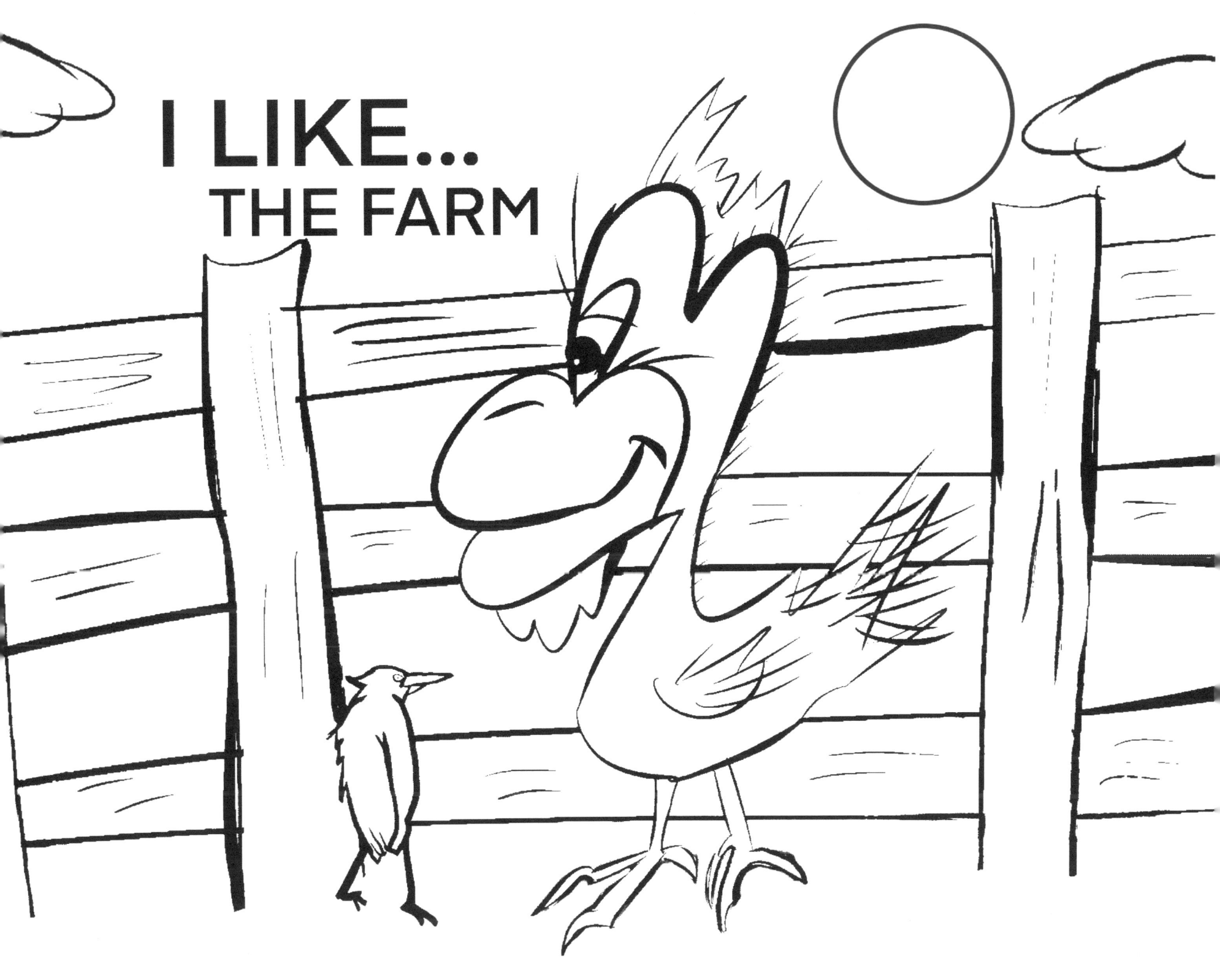

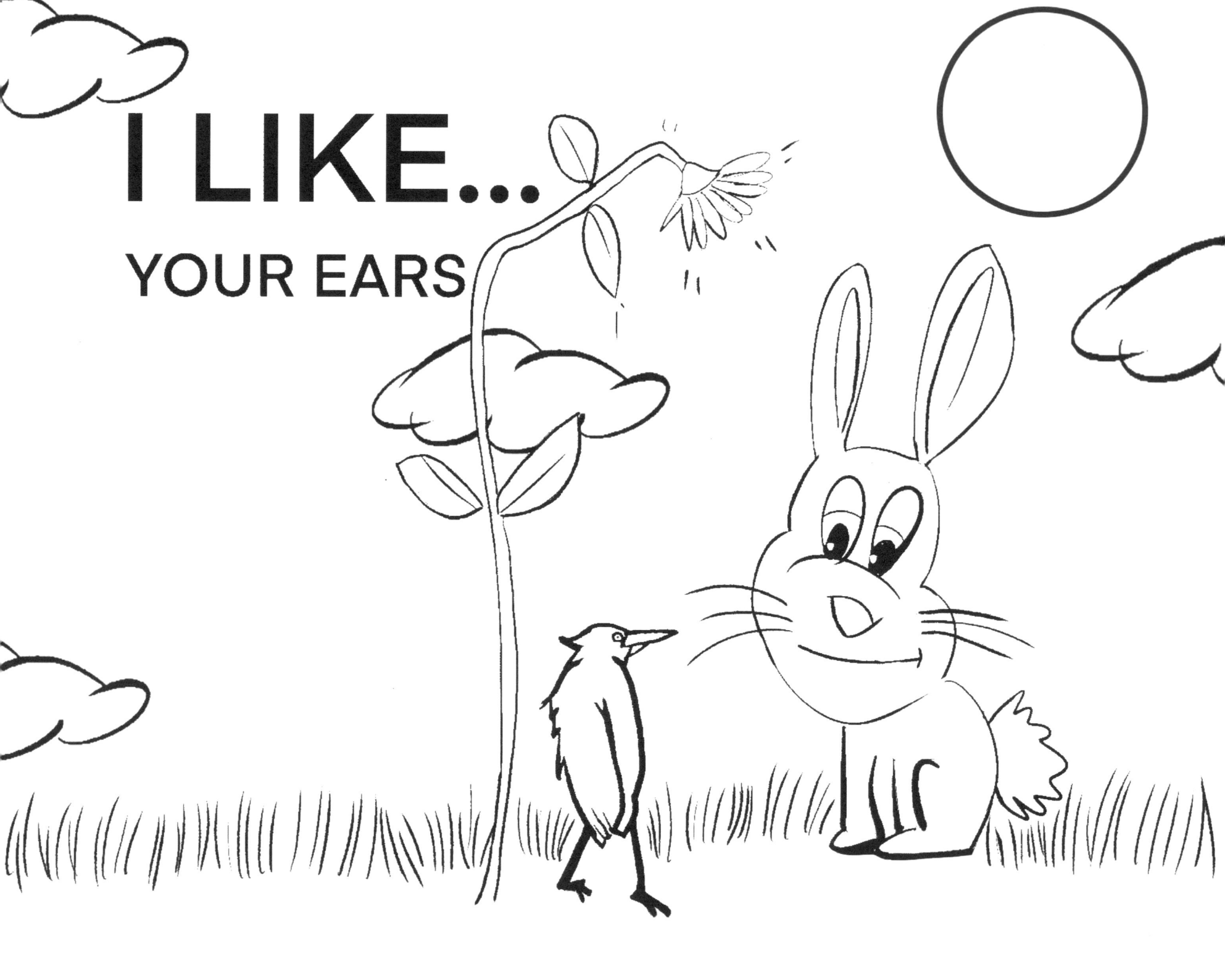

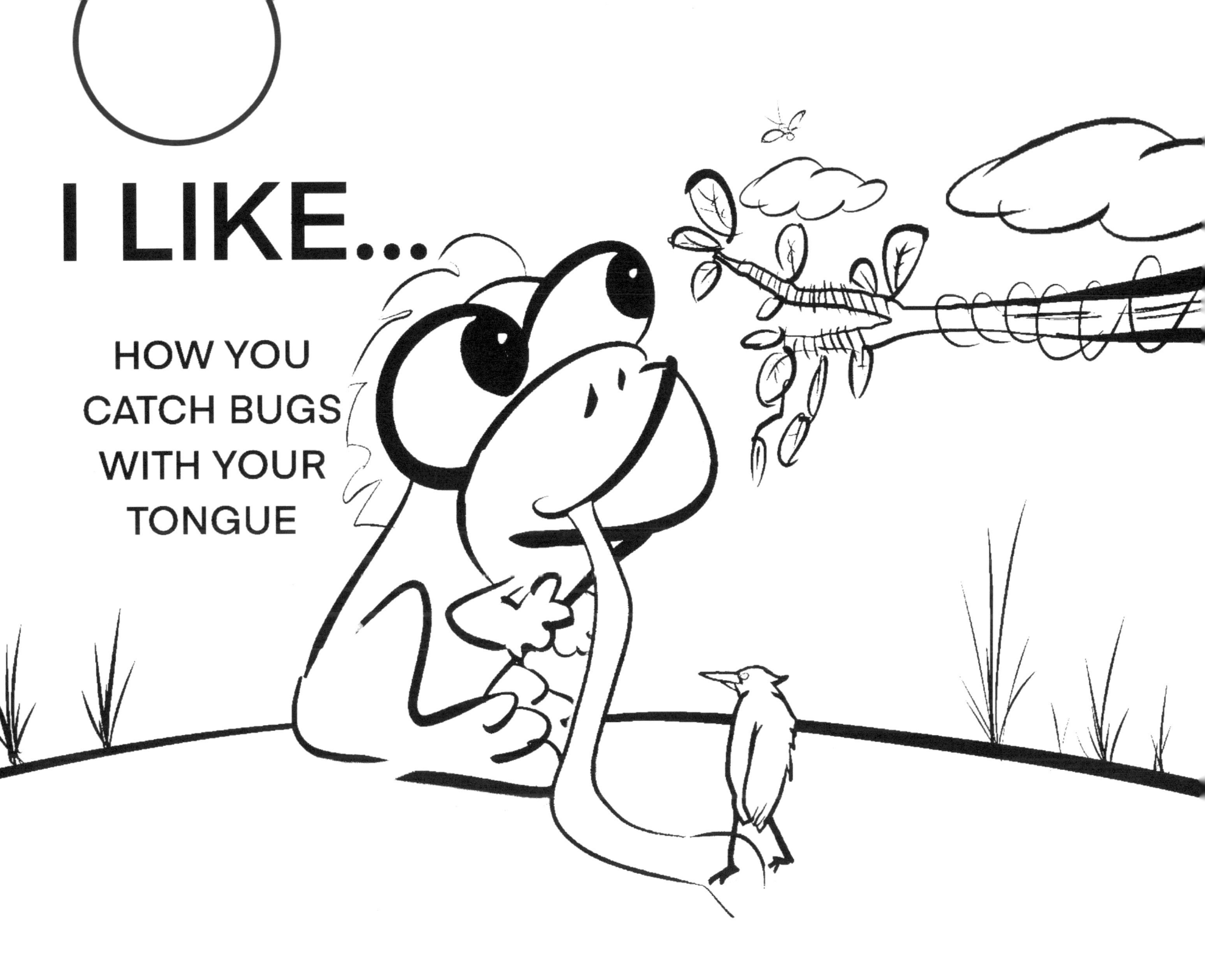

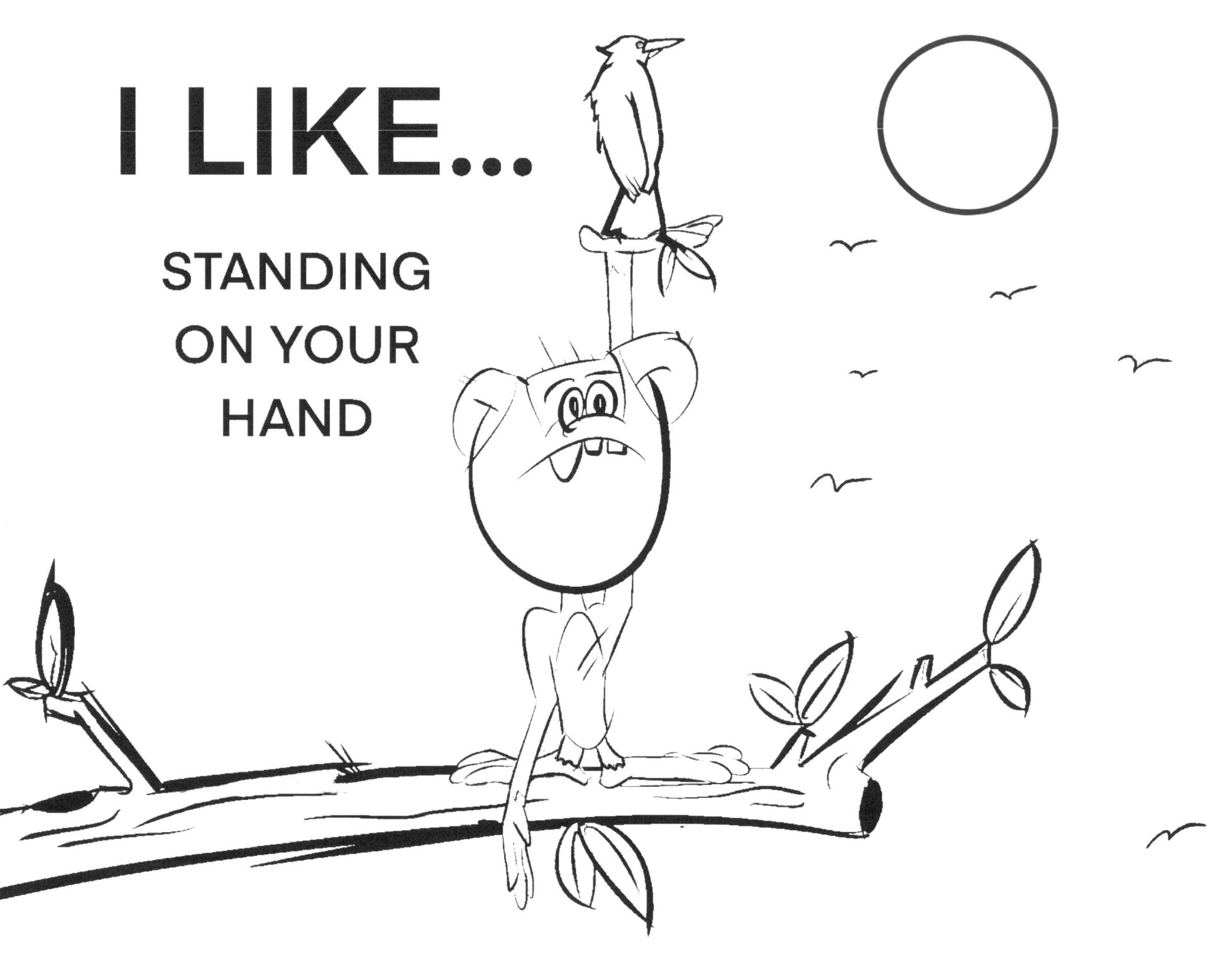

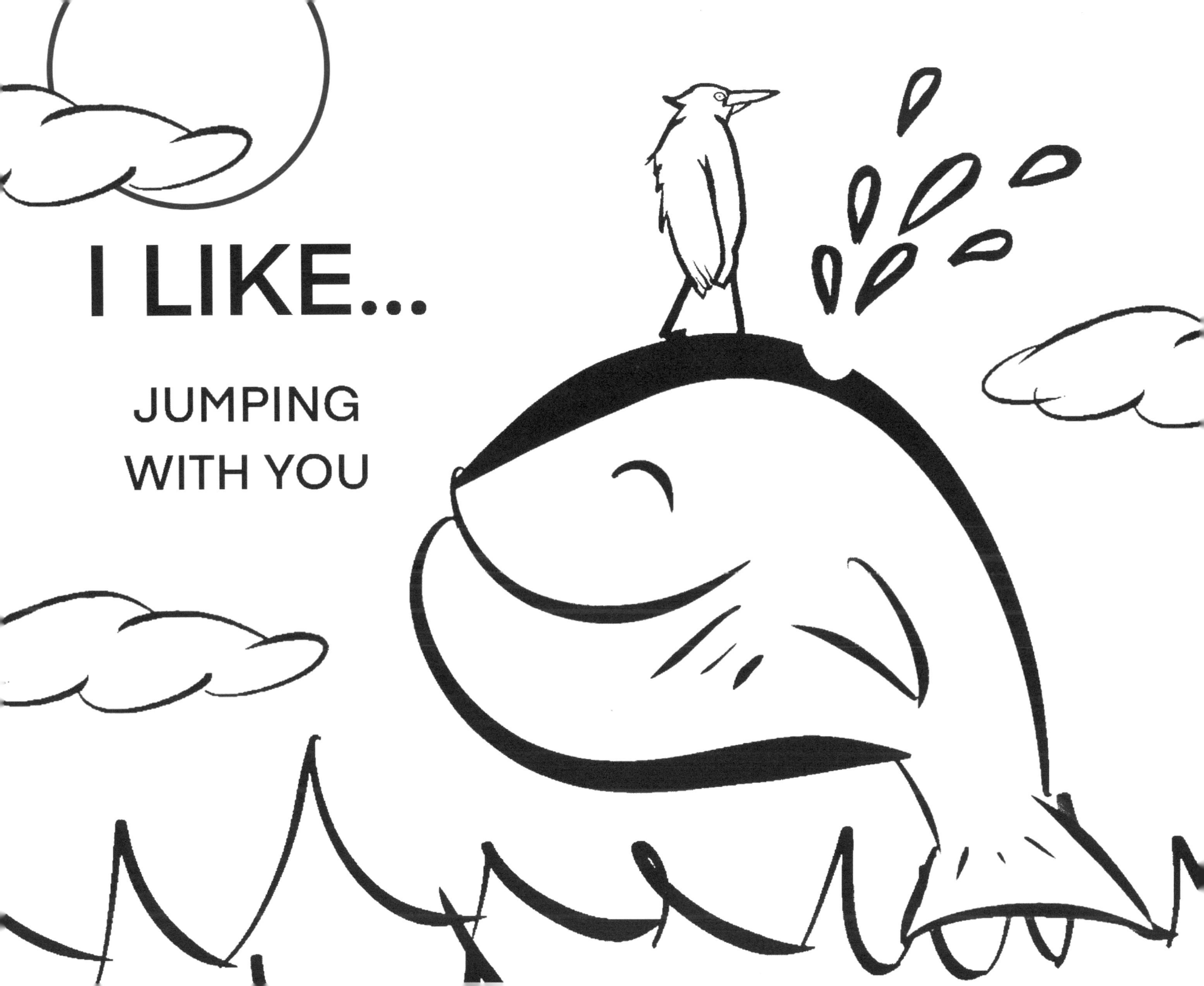

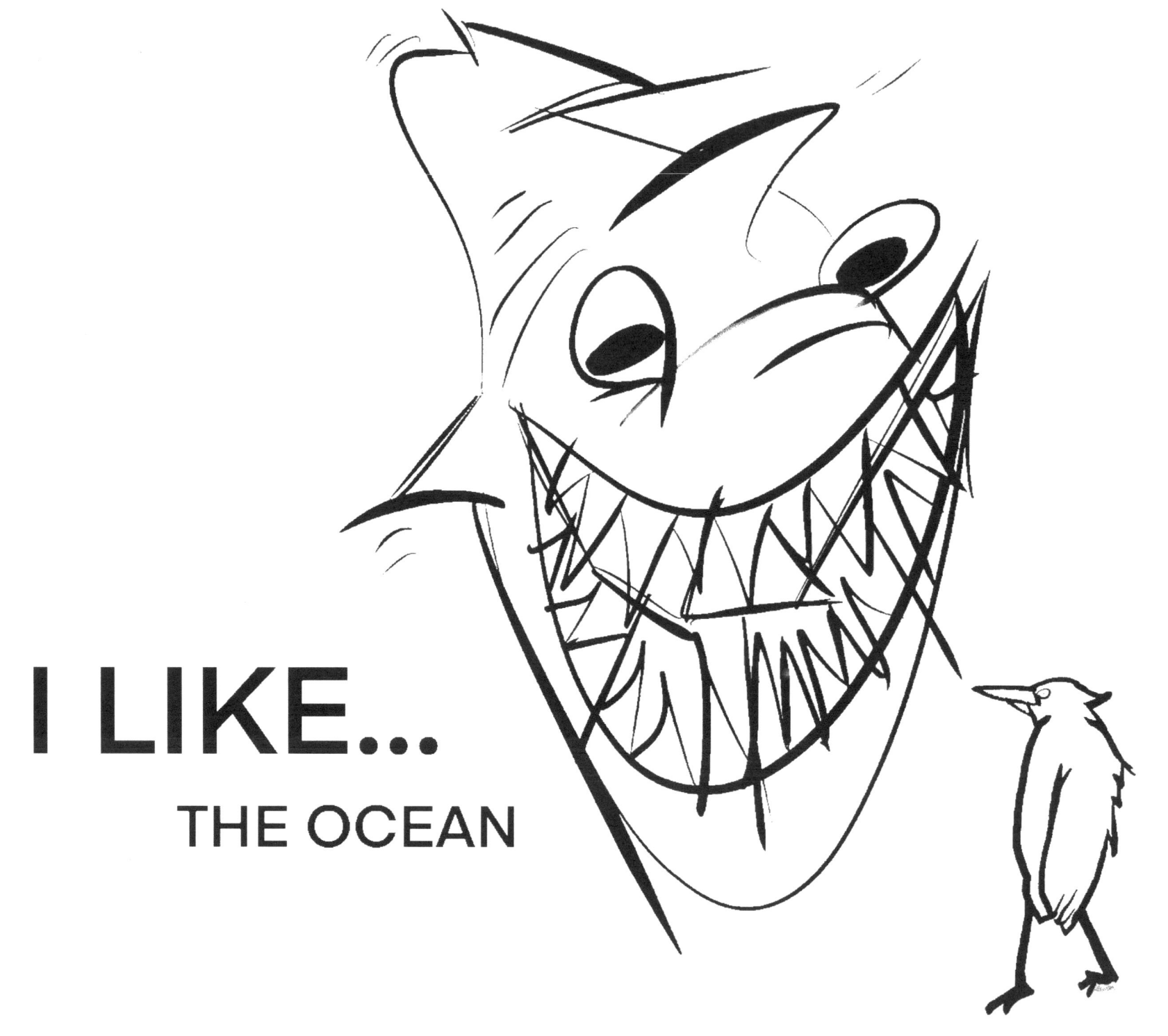

I LIKE...

THE OCEAN

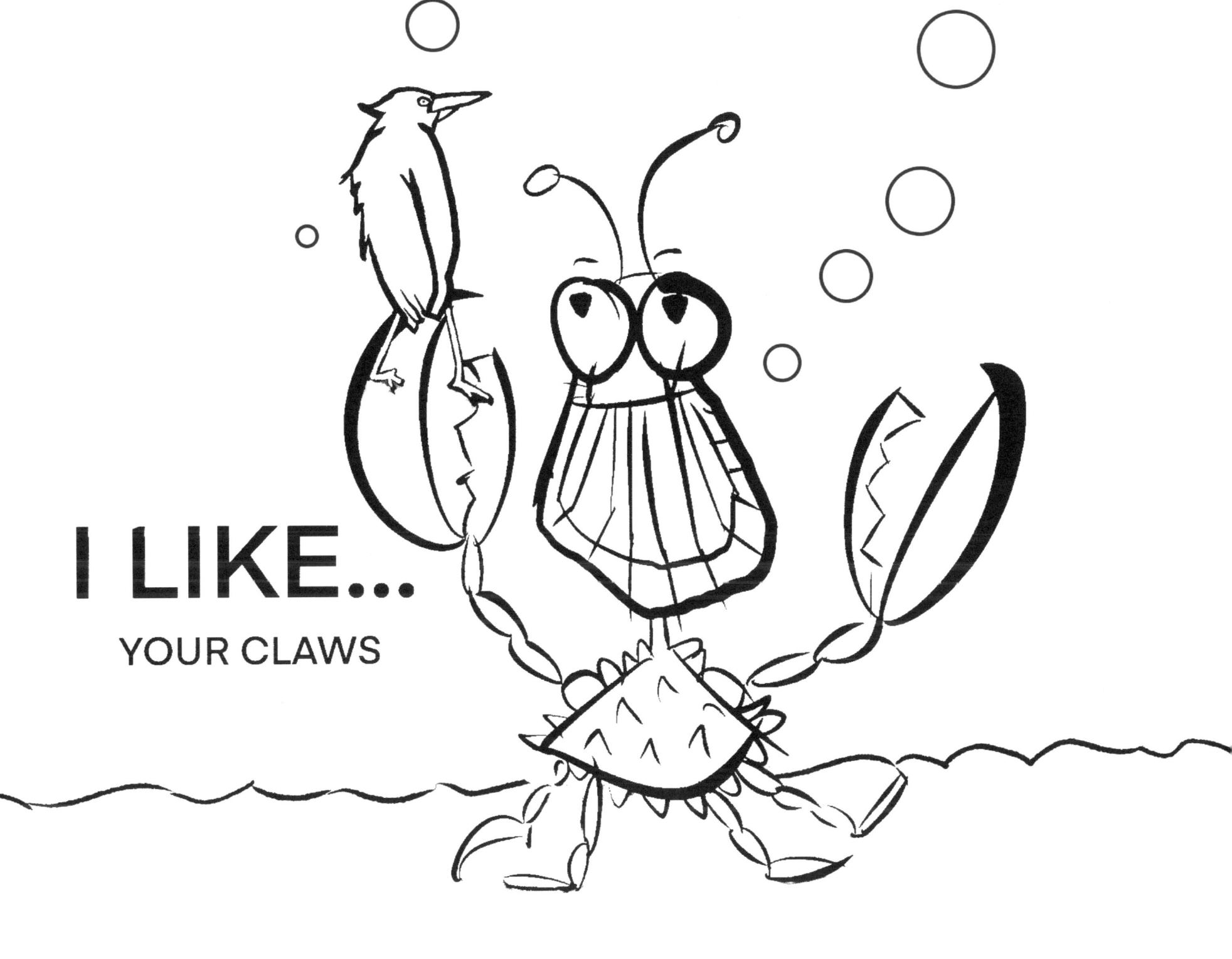

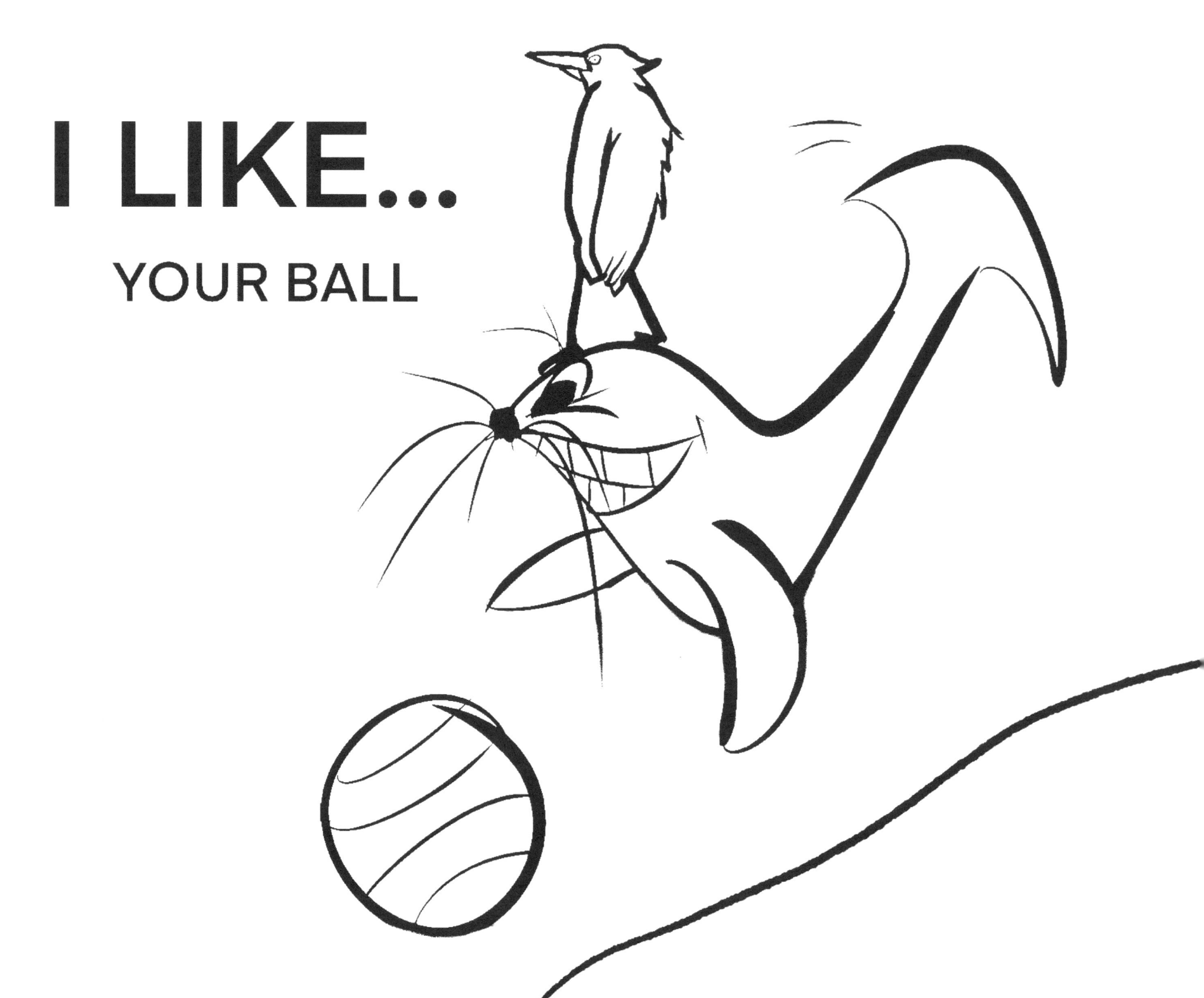

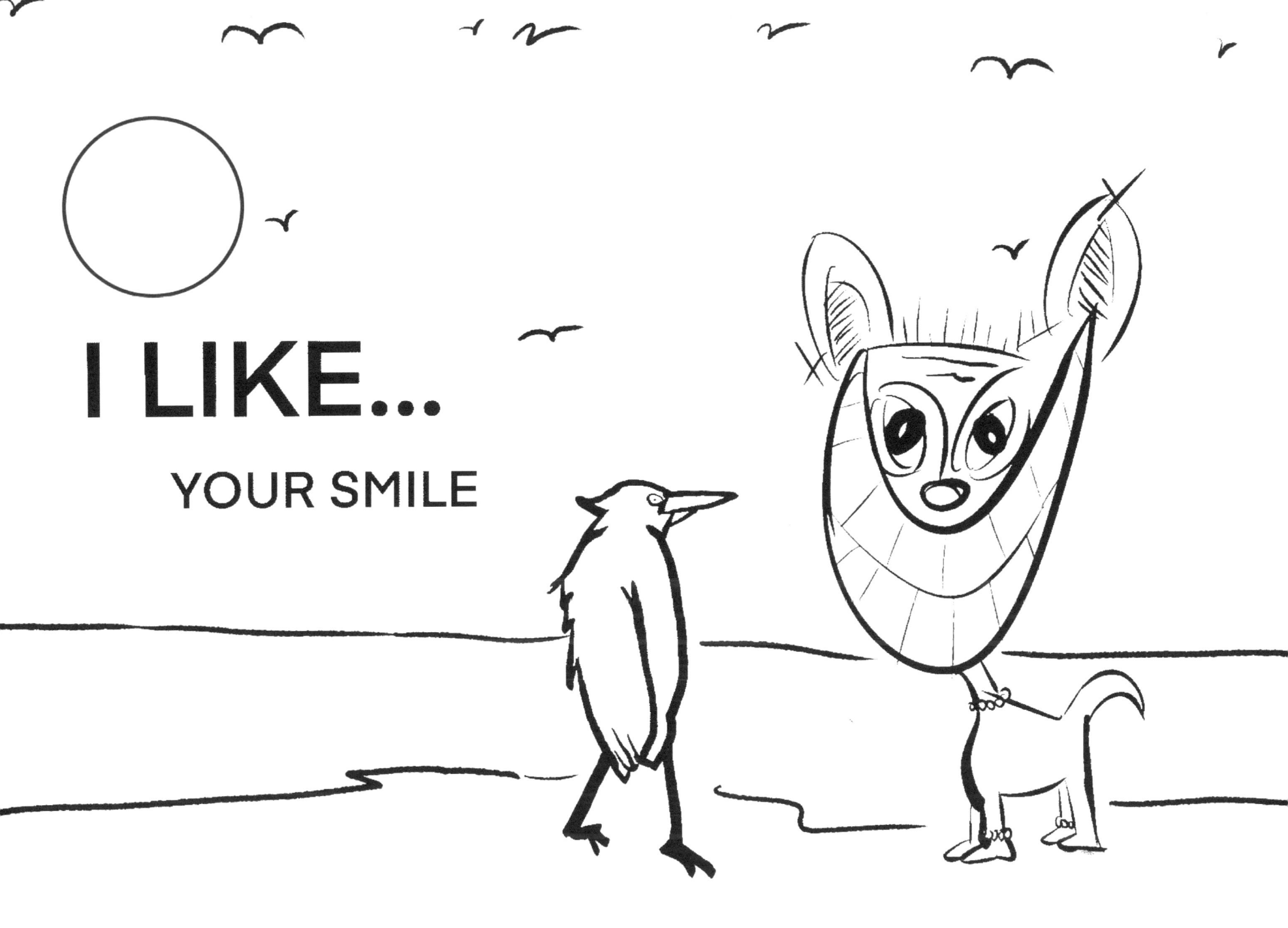

I LIKE...

VISITING YOU
IN THE FOREST

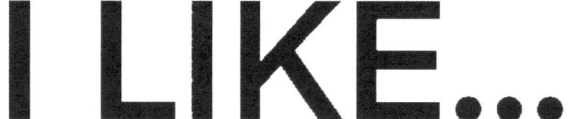

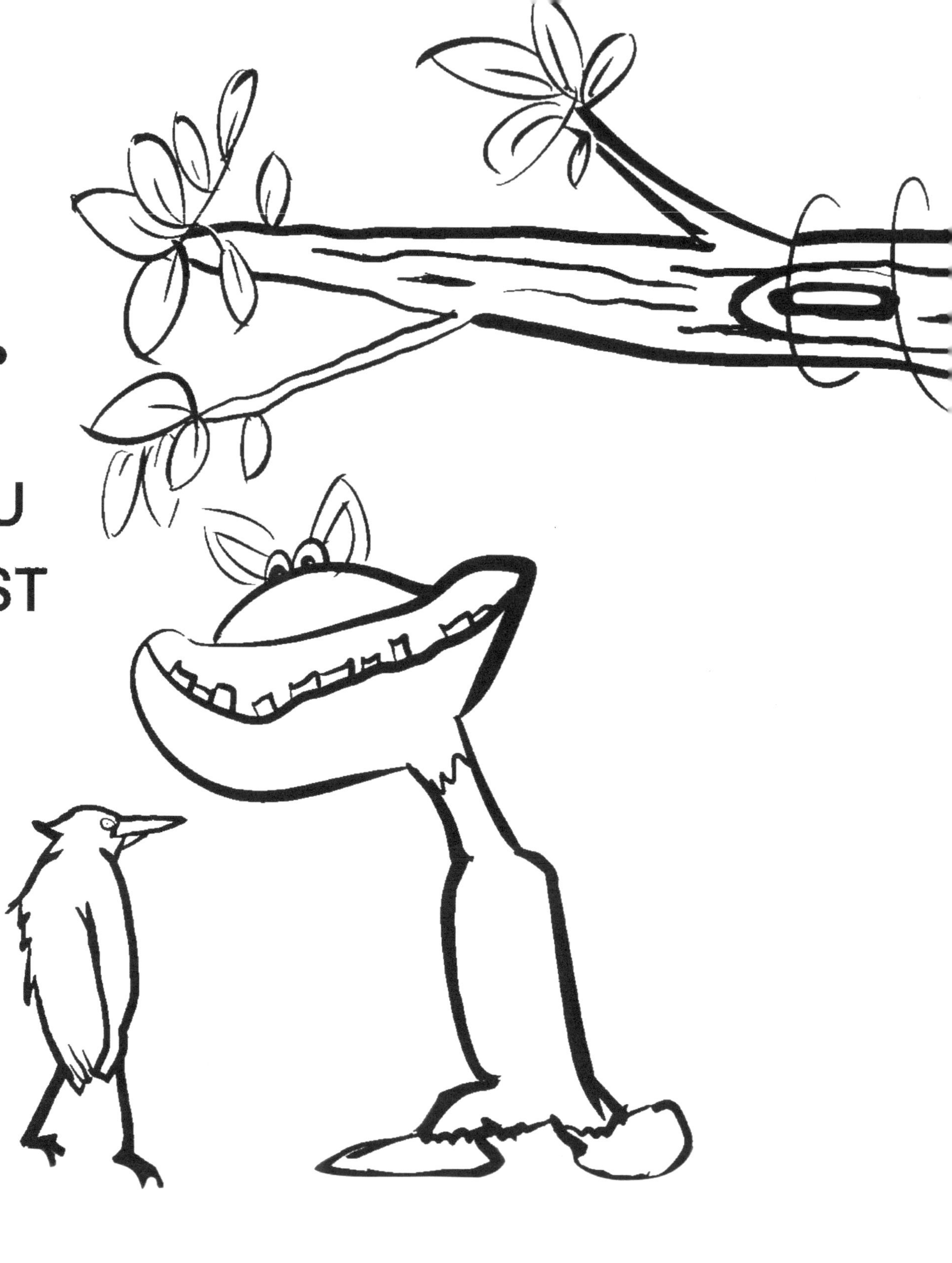

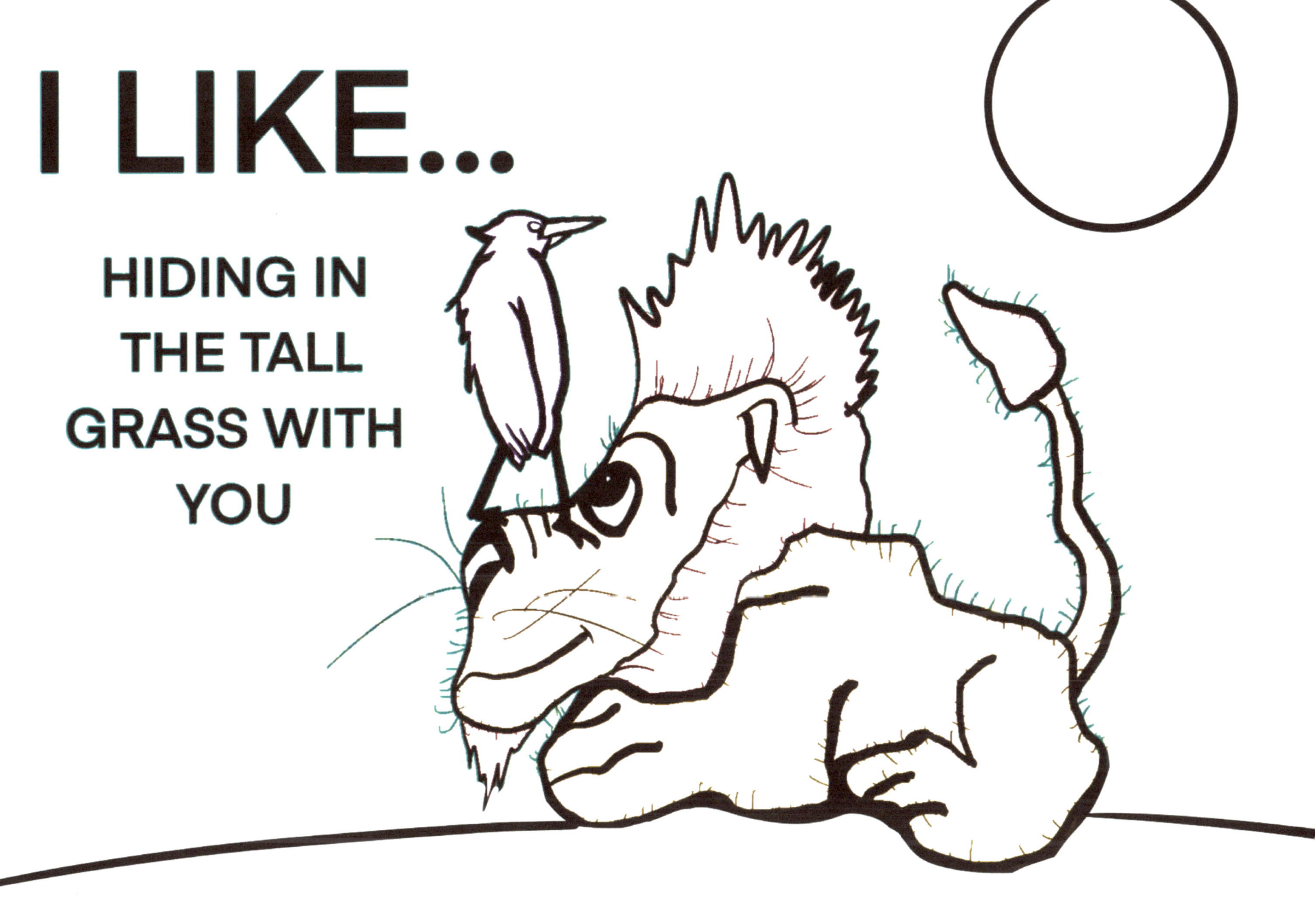

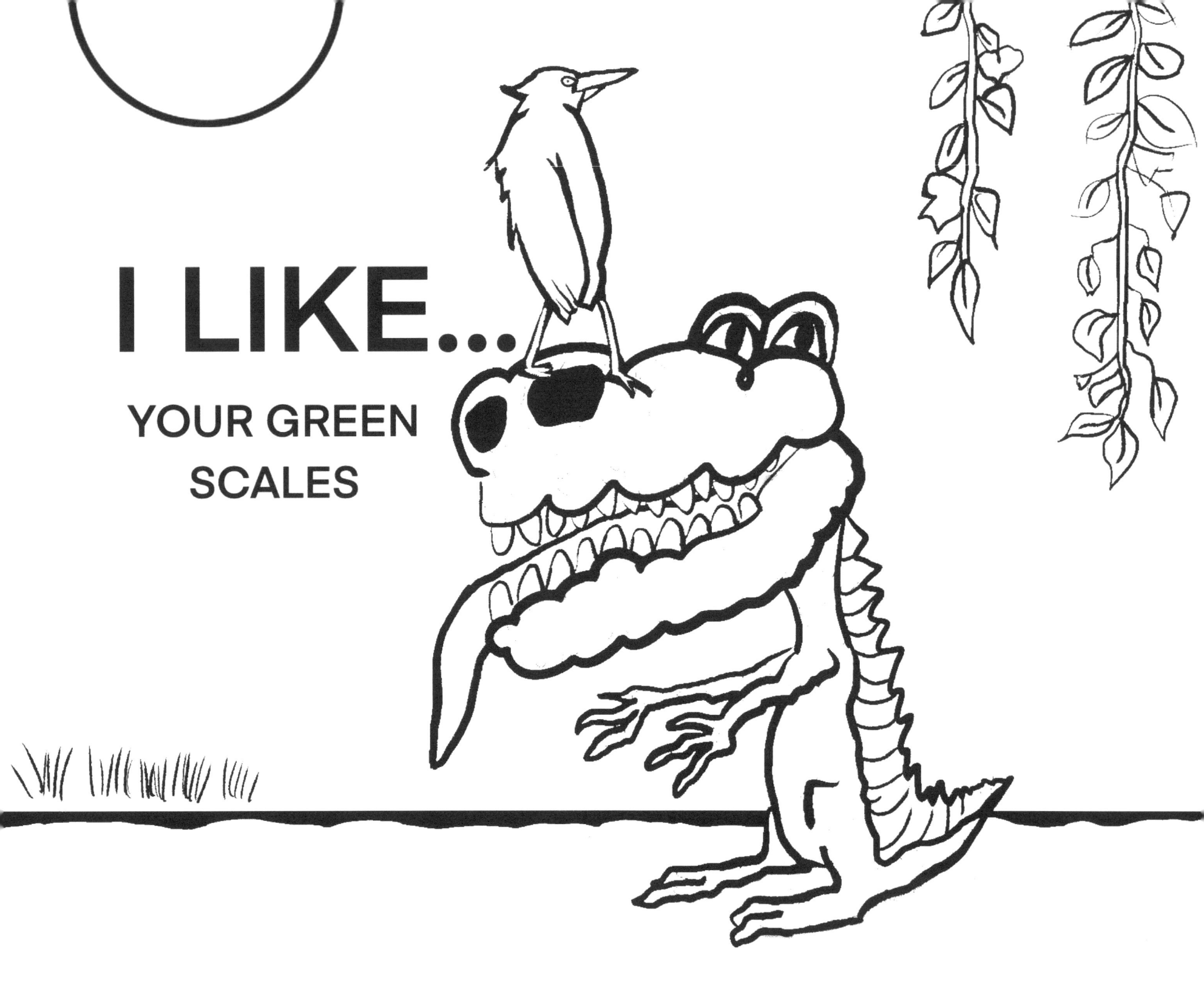

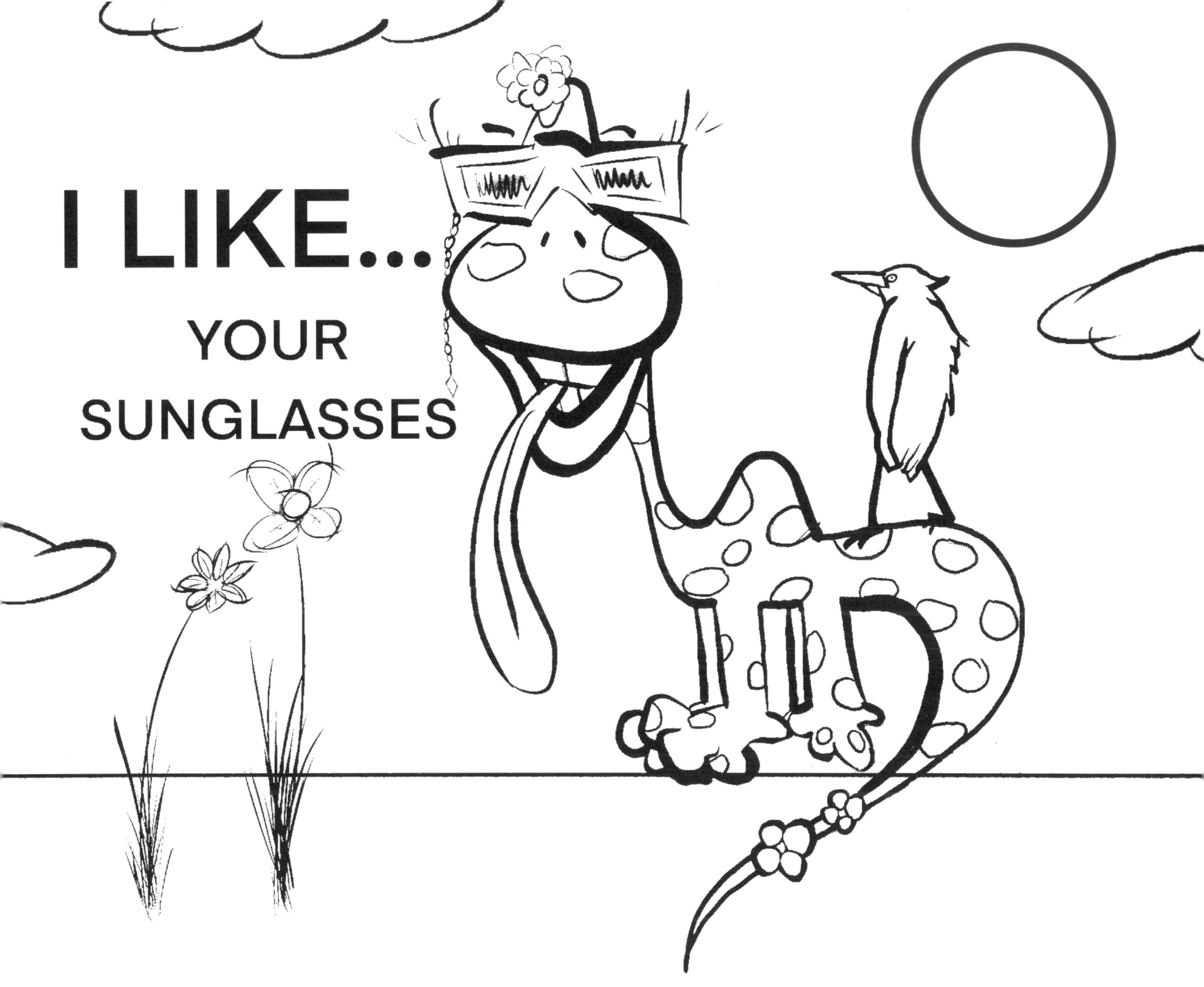

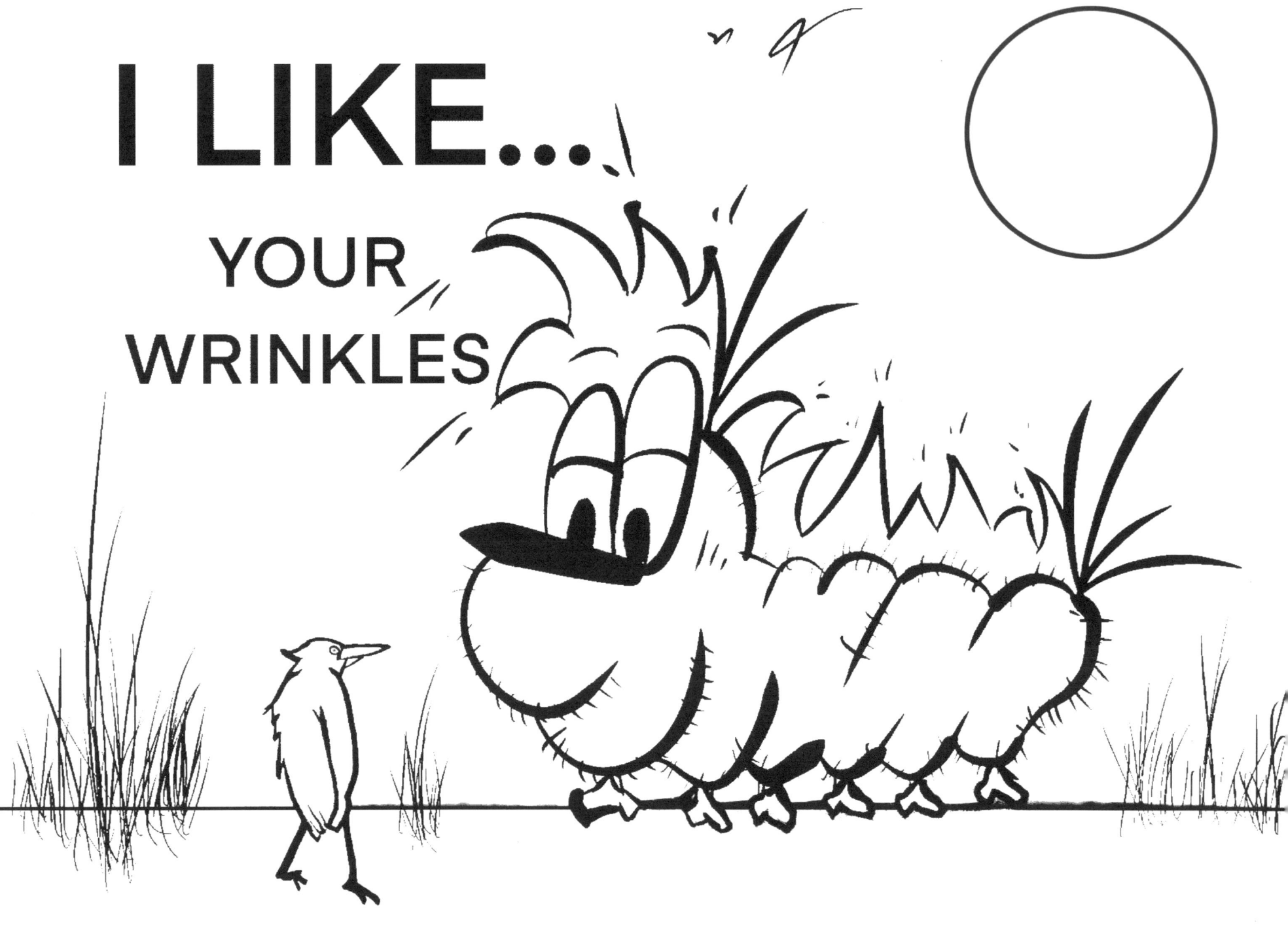

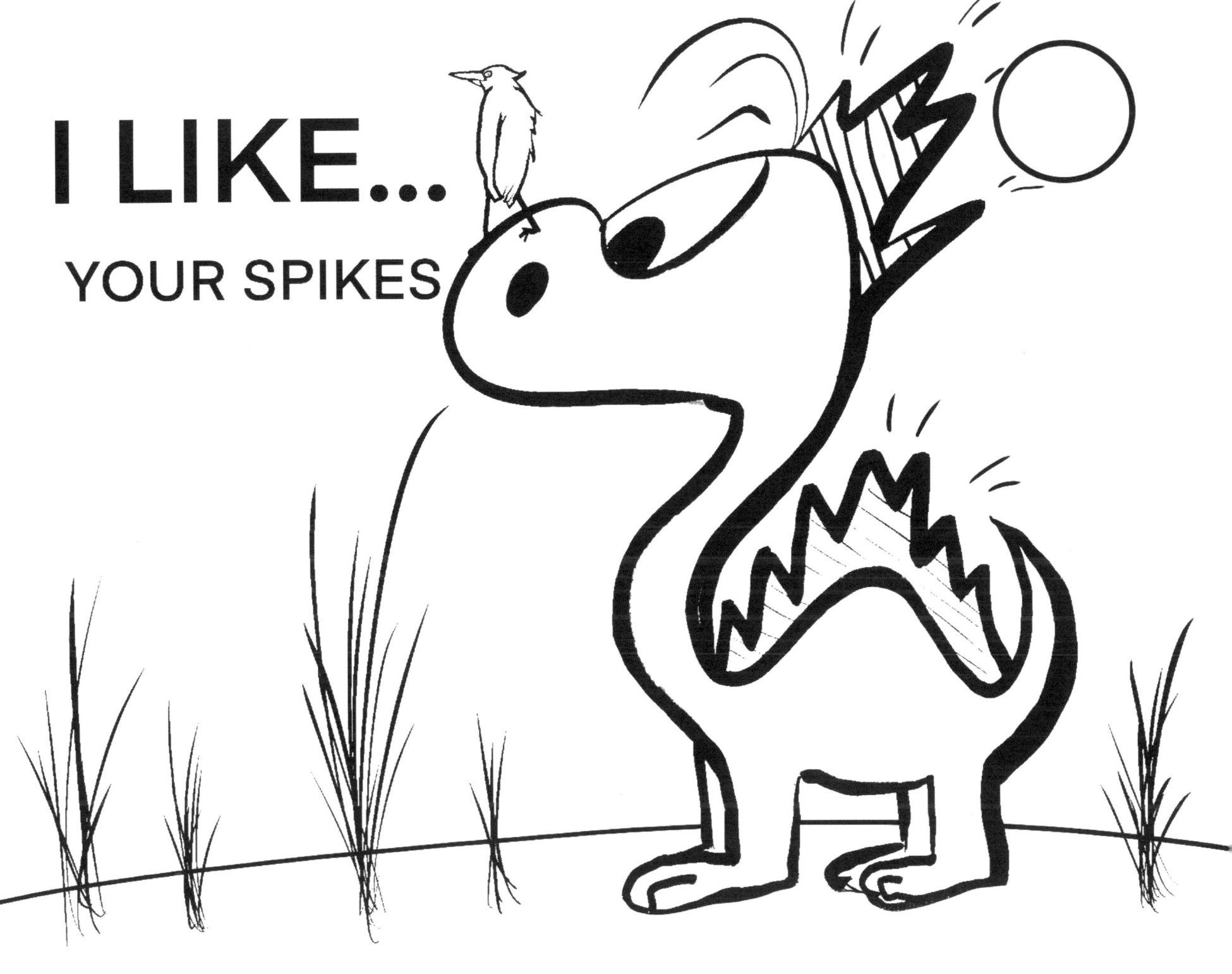

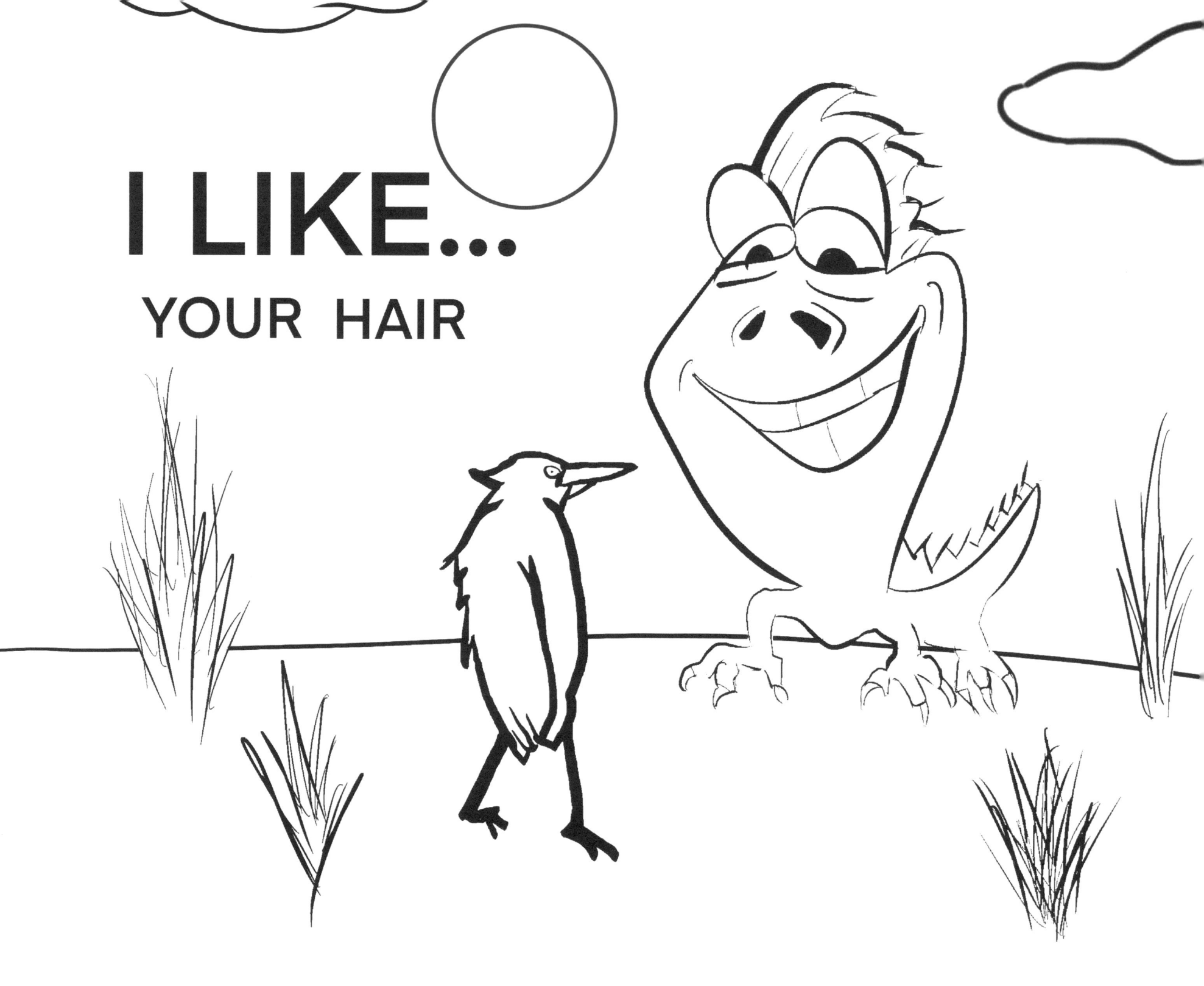

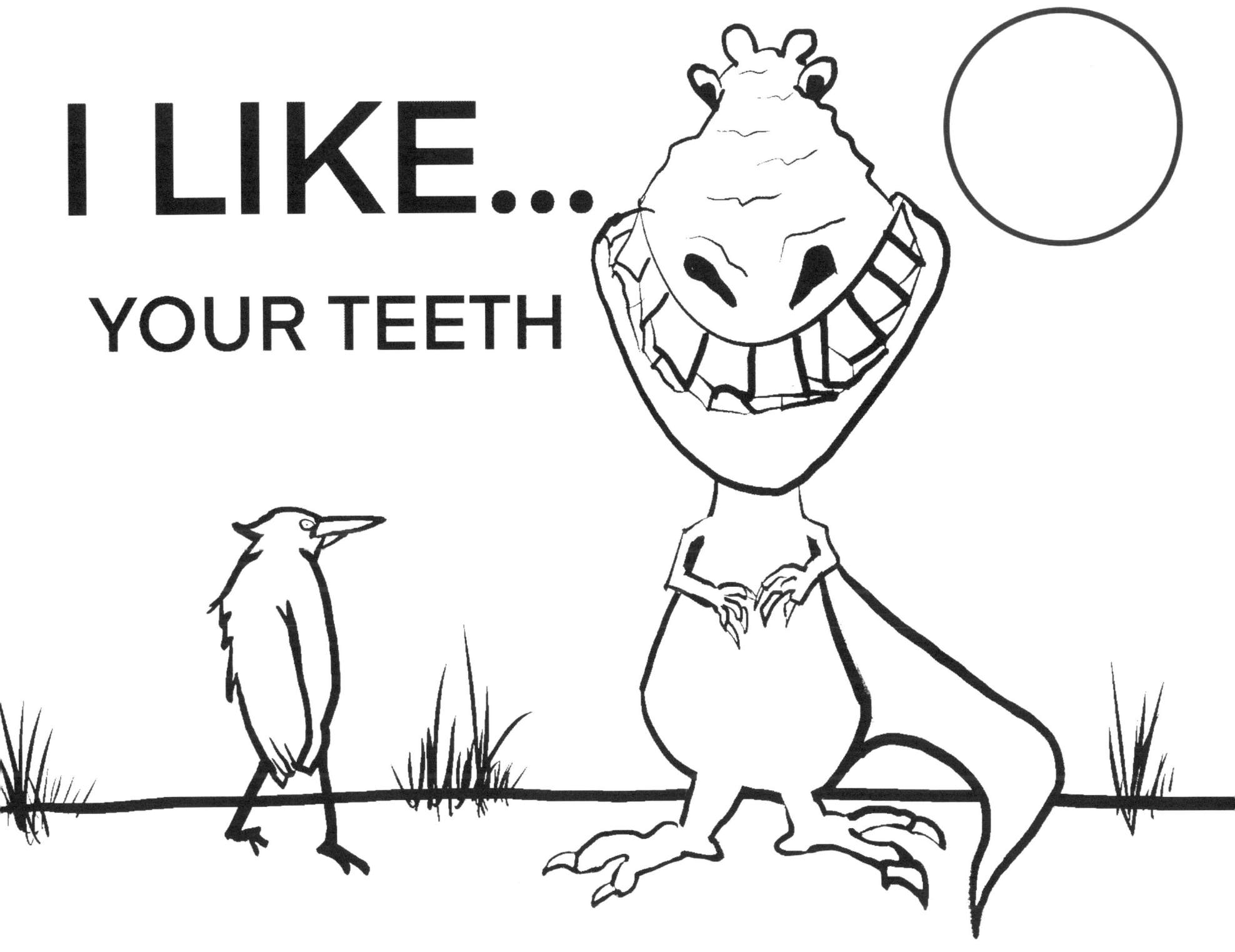

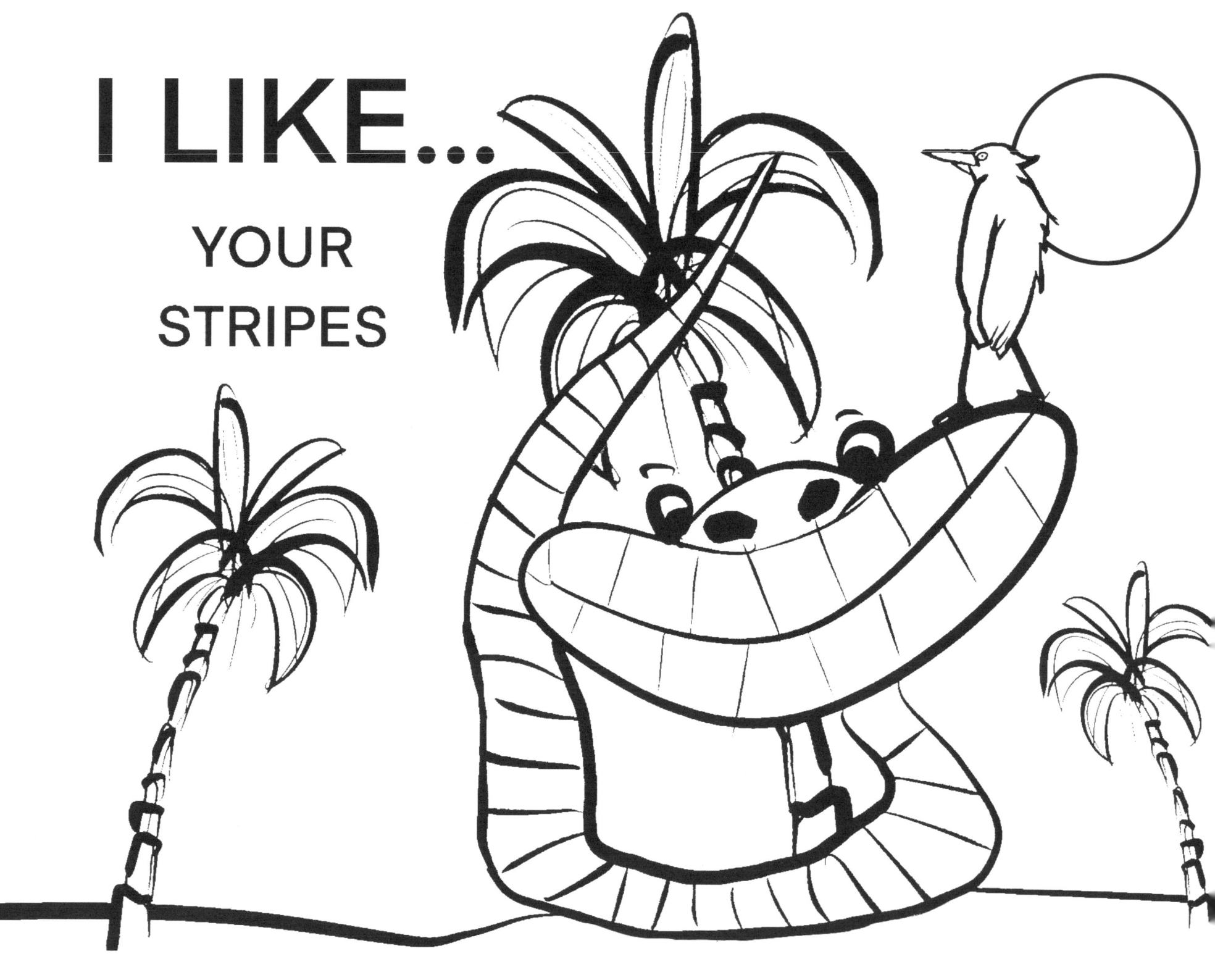

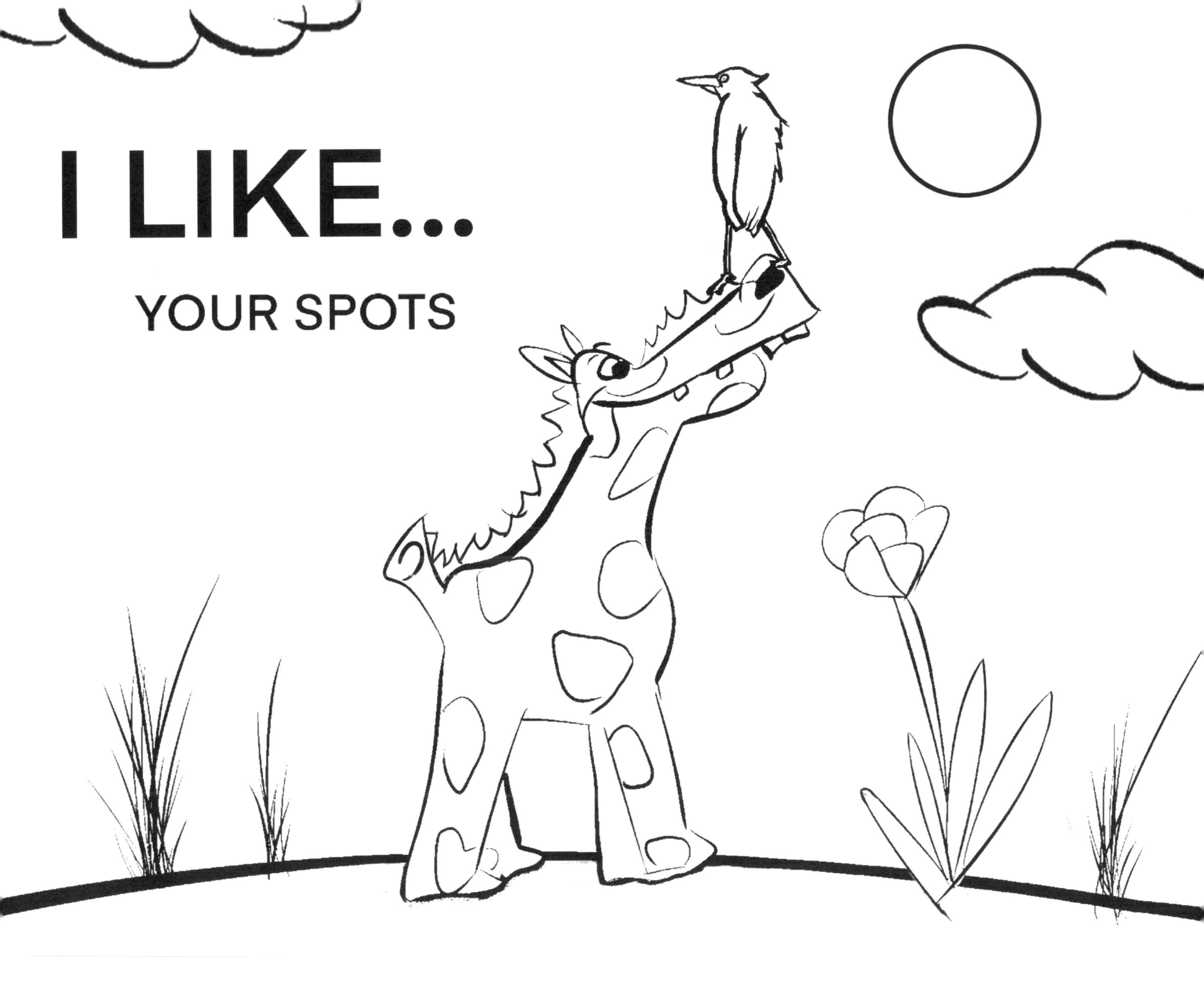

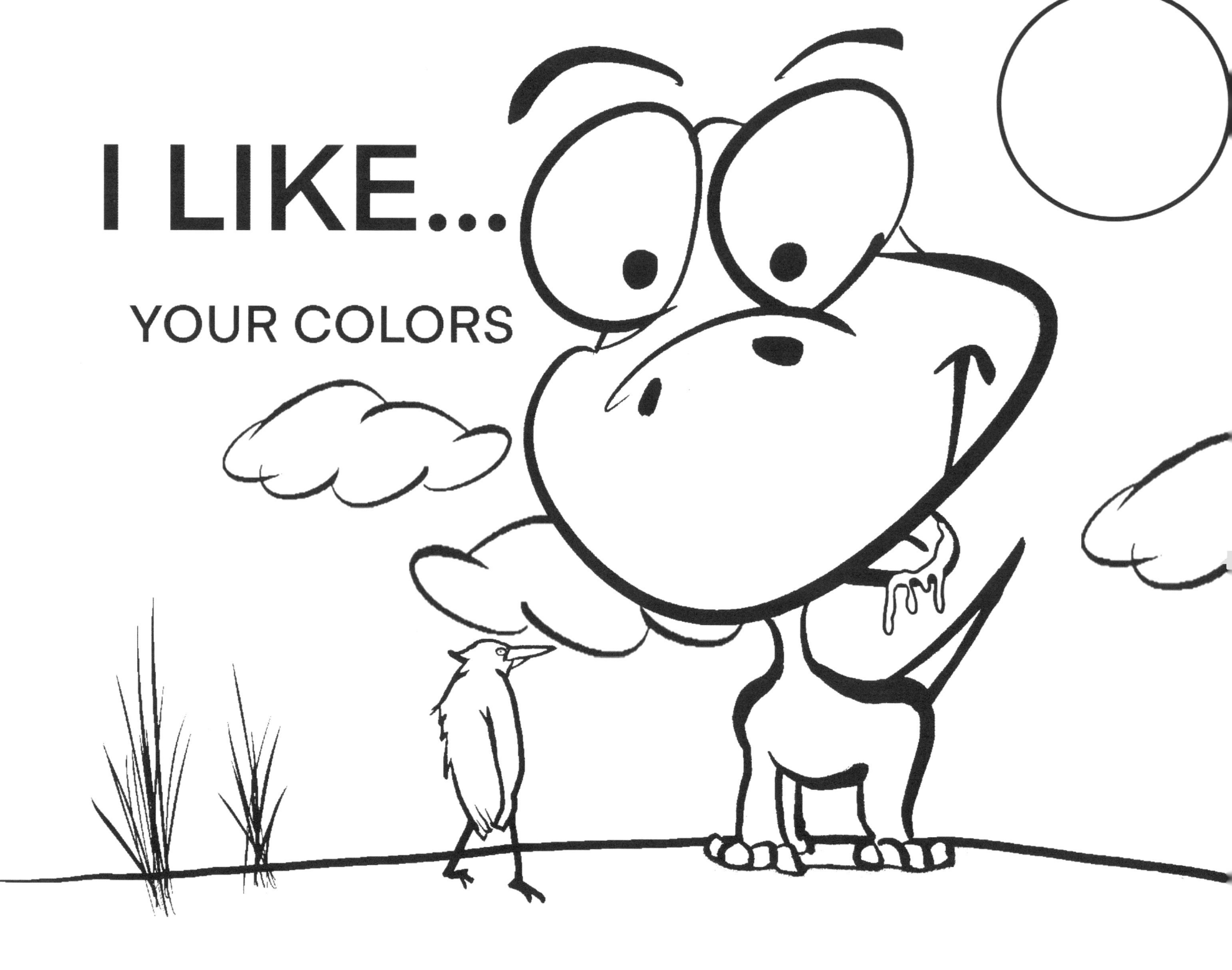

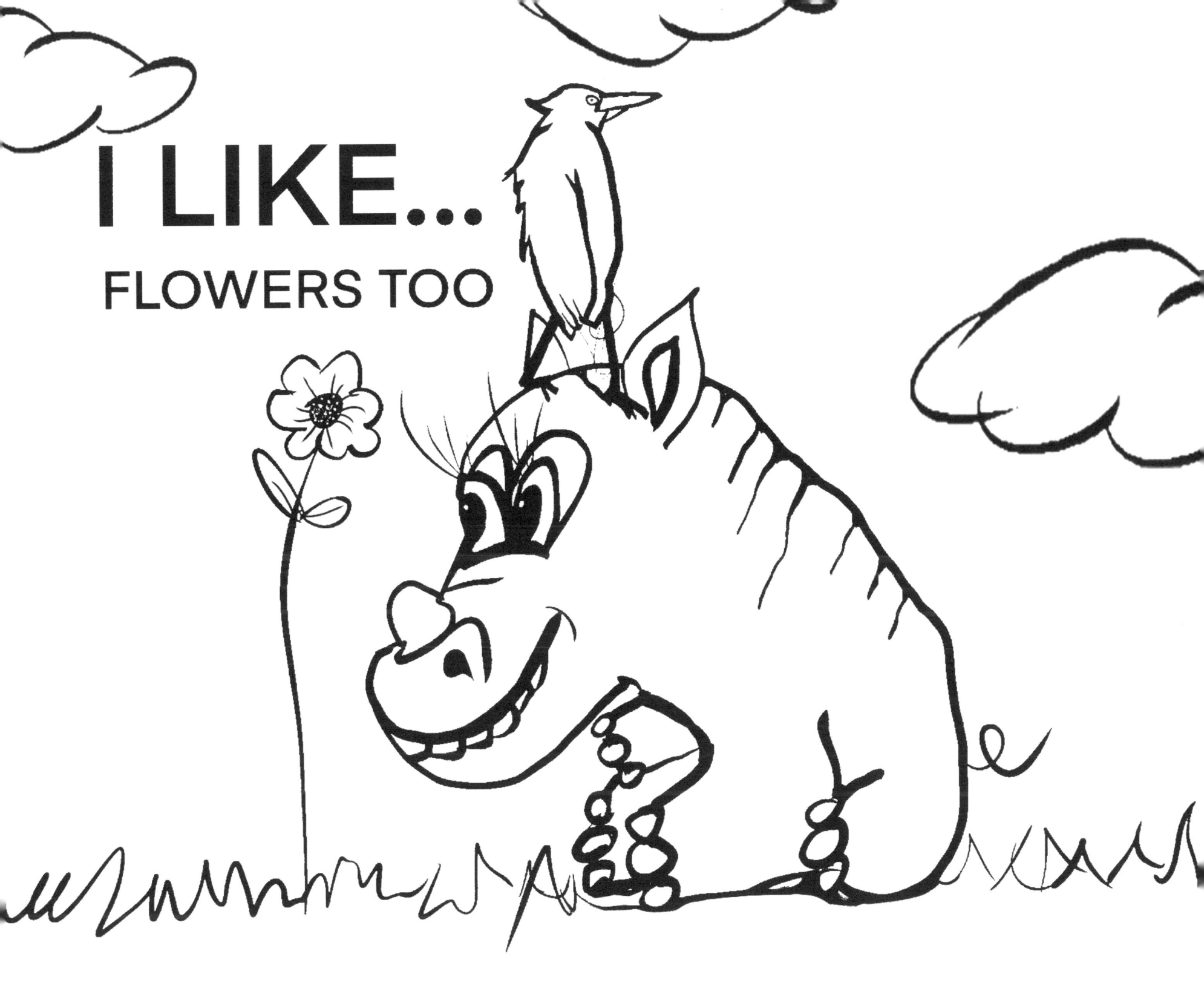

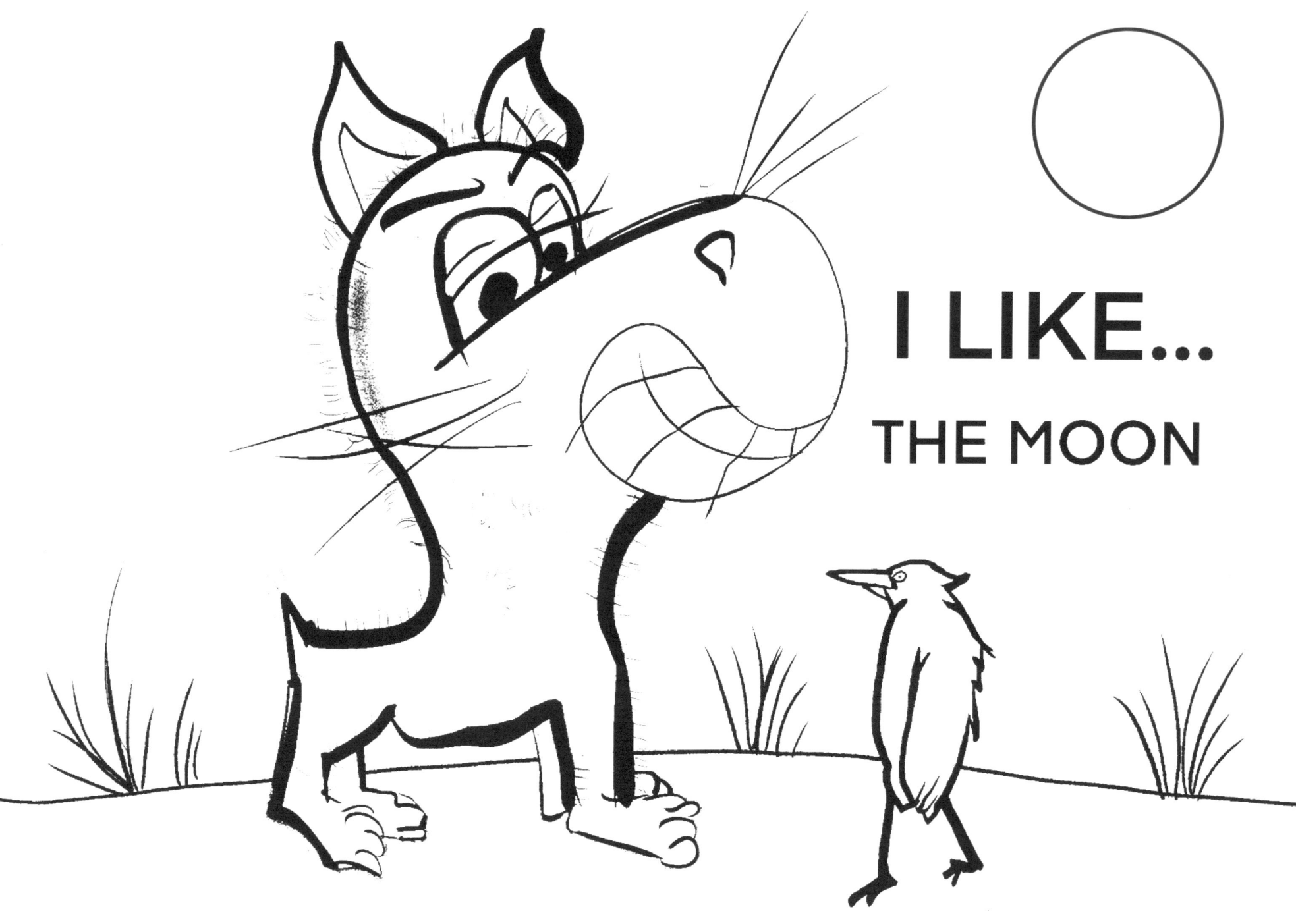

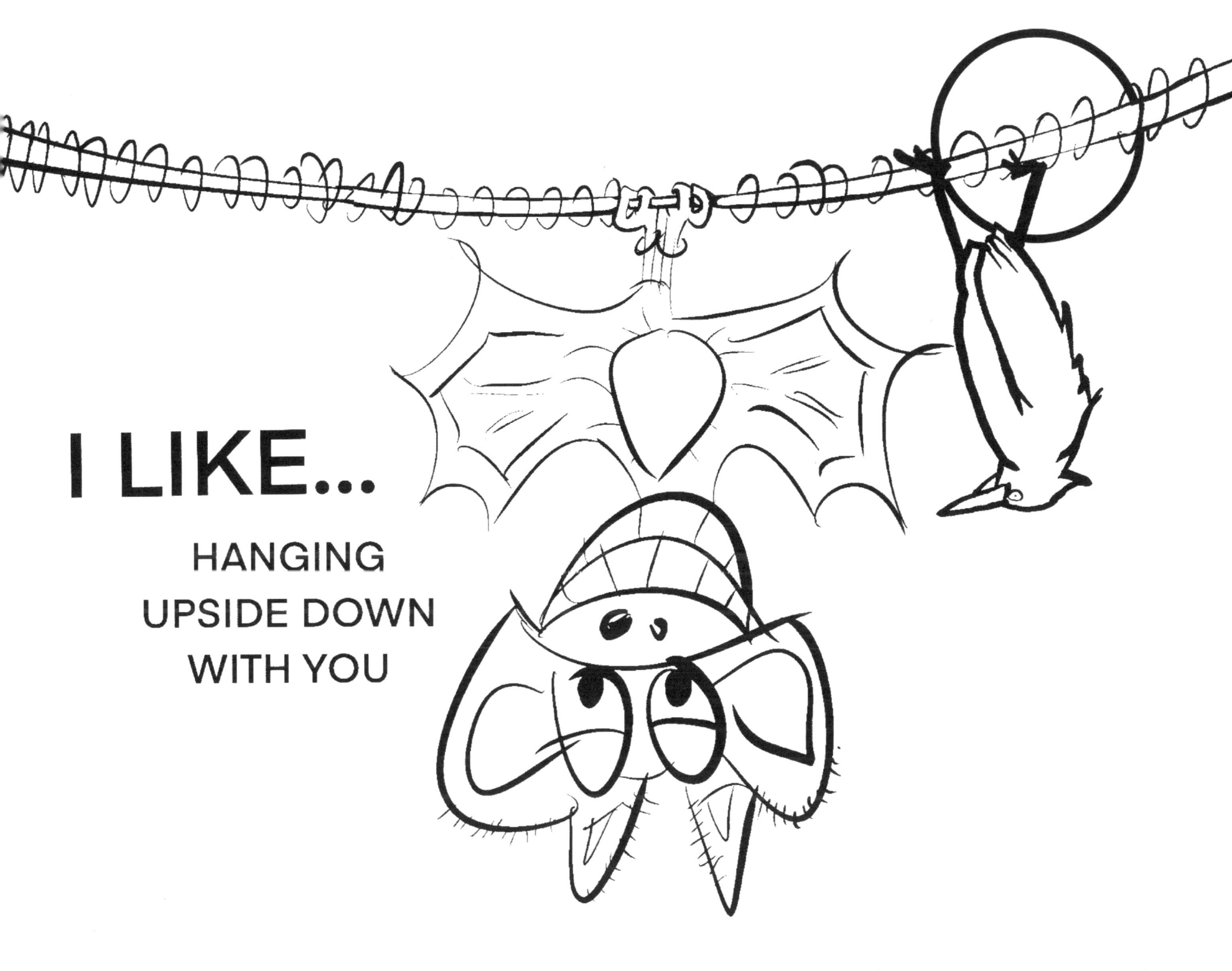

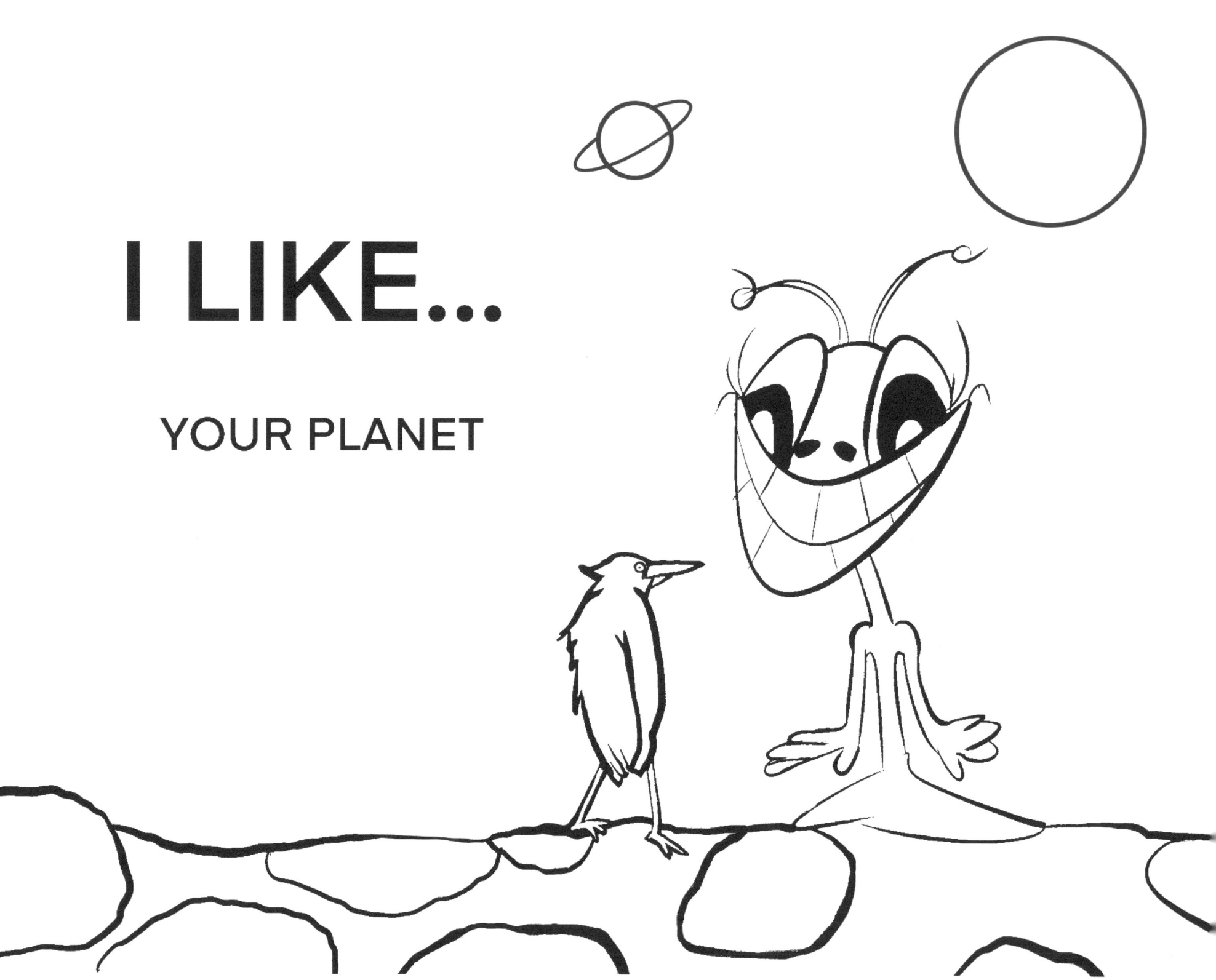

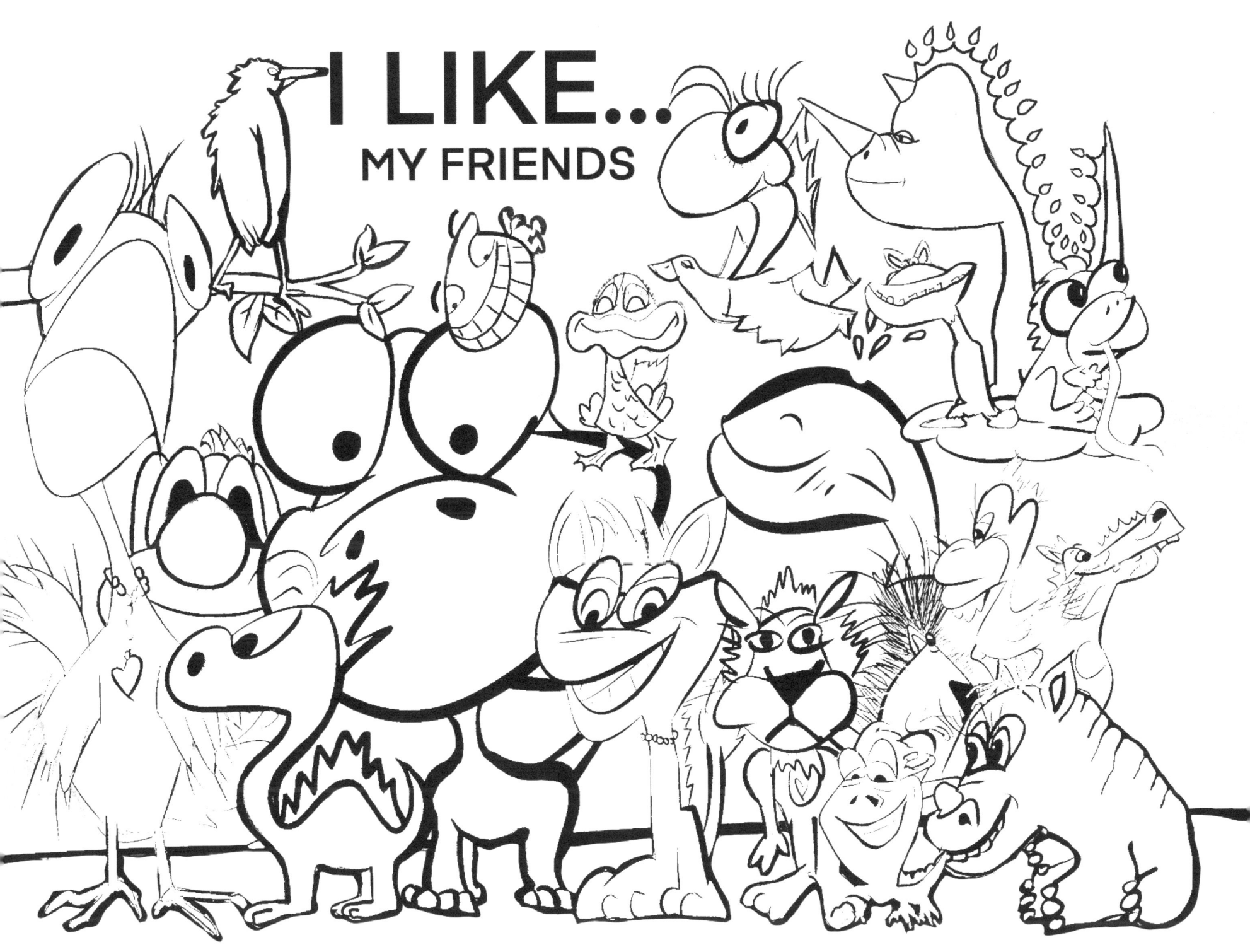

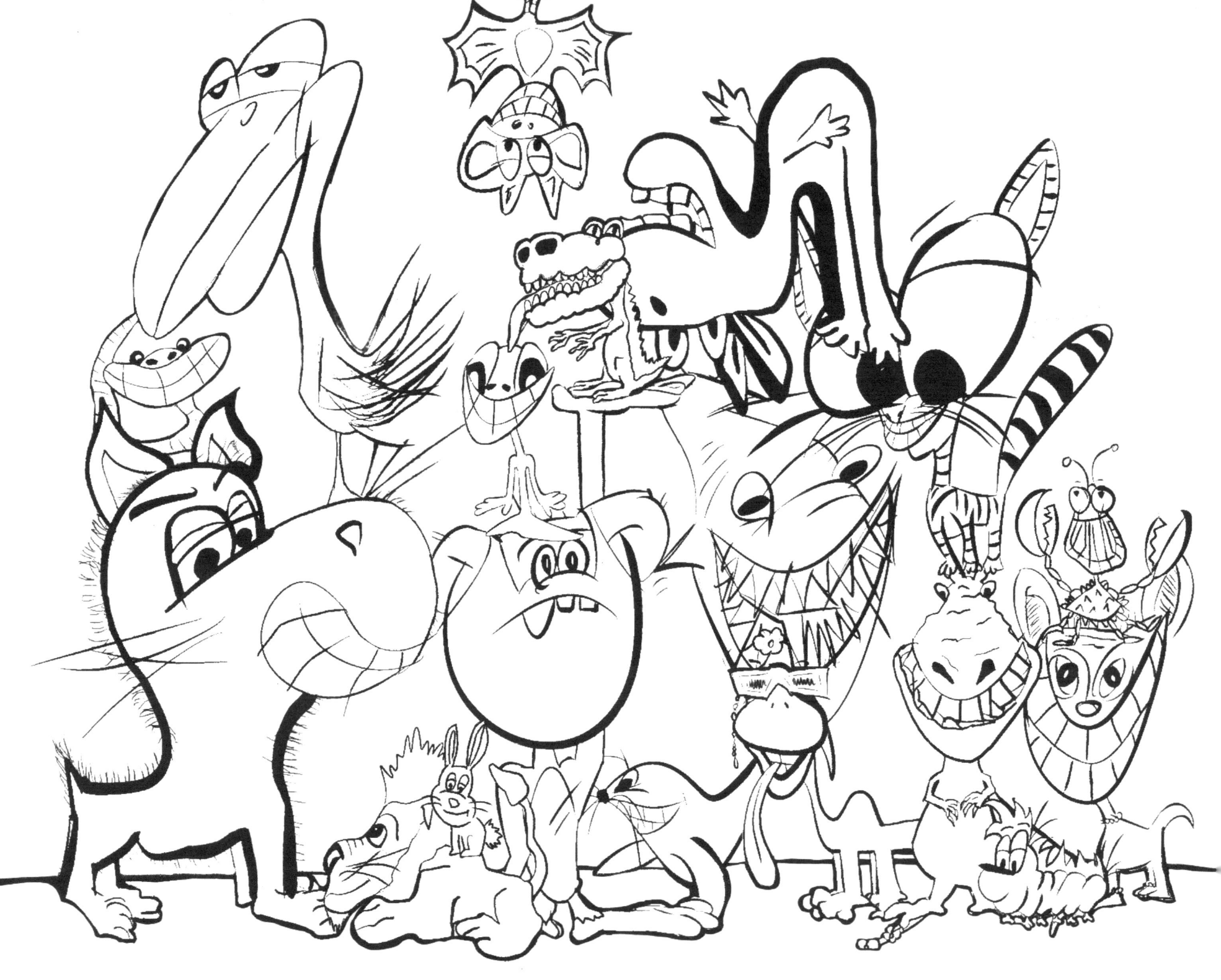

I LIKE...

SLEEP

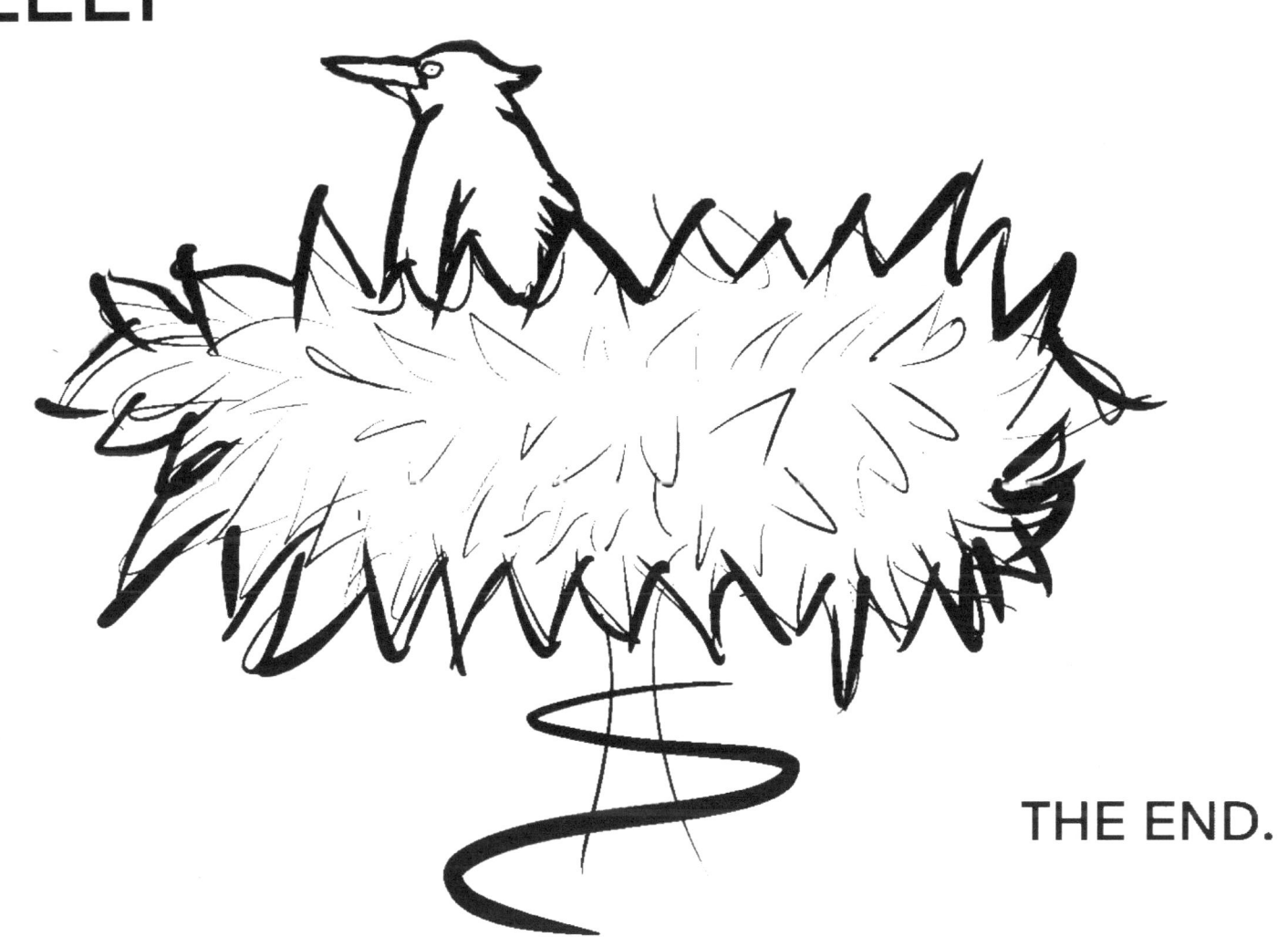

THE END.

Printed in the USA
CPSIA information can be obtained
at www.ICGtesting.com
LVHW071936110724

785246LV00005B/125